Enlightened

Little Boy Lost Series, Volume 1

JP Barnaby

Published by Recovery Romance Press, 2024.

ENLIGHTENED

First edition. November 15, 2024.

Copyright © 2024 JP Barnaby.

ISBN: 979-8230700784

Written by JP Barnaby.

Also by JP Barnaby

Little Boy Lost Series
Enlightened

The Survivor Series
Aaron
Ben
Spencer
Anthony
Sophie

Watch for more at www.jpbarnabyauthor.com.

Table of Contents

CHAPTER ONE

*M*y name is Brian Patrick McAllister and I am going to hell.

"In Romans one, verses twenty-four through twenty-eight, we find God calls these people and these acts that they perform unnatural—an abomination against Him. It says, 'Therefore God gave them over in the lusts of their hearts to impurity, so that their bodies would be dishonored among them, for they exchanged the truth of God for a lie and worshiped and served the creature rather than the Creator who is blessed forever'. Amen," the preacher cried, slamming his beefy hand onto the straining wood of the pulpit. In response, there was a resounding chorus of "Amen!" throughout the small congregation. I looked around and found that they were all, Jamie's mother included, enthralled by this charismatic, white-haired Baptist preacher. Even though they were fanning themselves or wiping their brows in the sweltering heat of the late southern Alabama morning, their attention never wavered.

The small tide of congregants, dressed in their Sunday finest, included men in short-sleeved button-downs and clip-on ties, as well as men in long sleeves and perfectly knotted standard-issue paisley ties. The women were almost clones of each other, most wearing gaudy floral dresses with perfectly respectable neck and hemlines that preserved their modesty. Their children were perfect little carbon copies of their parents, with one glaring exception: these miniature adults in their ties and floral dresses seemed to be bored almost senseless.

Taking a deep breath that nearly popped the straining buttons on his starched white dress shirt, the preacher continued reading from his large hardcover Bible, encouraged by his followers' enthusiastic responses. "For this reason, God gave them over to degrading passions. For their women exchanged the natural function for that which is unnatural and in the same way also the men abandoned the natural function of the woman and burned'—notice, folks, that it says burned—'in their desire toward one another, men with men committing indecent acts and receiving in their own persons the dire penalty of their error. And just as they did not see fit to acknowledge God any longer, God gave them over to a depraved mind to do those things which are not proper!'"

The thunderous sound of him slamming his Bible closed against the wood jarred me, and I jerked in my seat. Jamie looked at me, concerned, but after meeting his eye for the briefest second, I looked away. He seemed so angelic in his light-blue button-down and dress pants, his blond hair falling into his eyes. Because of the heat, Mrs. Mayfield had let him skip the tie, and I could see the smooth skin of this throat behind his open collar. My stomach lurched, and my mind and my heart were both racing. How I felt about Jamie, I was everything that the preacher was ranting about: depraved, indecent, and immoral. Jamie Mayfield was my best friend in the world, and I wanted him more than anything else in it.

I looked up again at the giant of a man in his threadbare sky-blue Sunday suit. He was using a white narrow-brimmed hat to fan his sweaty, flushed face. The excitement blazed in his eyes. He was passionate about his sermon, and he truly believed in everything that he preached. Had his words really come from God? The preacher loosened his dark blue patterned tie, just enough to reveal the top of his neatly buttoned shirt to the captivated audience. No clip-on tie for this man; he was the real deal, the embodiment of Southern grace.

The pulpit where he tended and shepherded his flock was old but lovingly maintained. While the worn wood no longer gleamed in the morning sun, it was spotless, without even a wayward scratch. The large, perfectly crisp engraved cross on the front nearly glowed from its recent waxing and polishing. If everything in the world had its place, this was certainly the preacher's place. He was perfectly at home, frightening as he was, and comfortable in his element, addressing the Sunday crowd from his old wooden pedestal.

As his sermon came to a close, I thought about what he'd said. For a few years now, I had tried not to enjoy looking at other boys, instead forcing myself to think about girls when I lay in bed at night jacking off. I thought about the half-naked, faceless girls that I'd seen on television. I thought about their bare silicone-infused breasts, naked hips and thighs, and tight asses in their jeans. Sometimes, I even used hand lotion from my foster mother's bathroom to make it feel all slick and wet, as I imagined a girl would feel. I was fairly certain my use of her lotion would have disgusted Carolyn.

But when it came down to it, when I was so fucking horny that my mind disengaged from my conscious fantasies, when those random images shot through my head, there was only one thing that I would see. My imagination focused completely on the shaggy mop of blond hair, mischievous blue eyes, and skinny body of a seventeen-year-old boy. I imagined my best friend in the world as his lips closed around me. I could almost feel his soft blond hair brushing against my stomach, his faintly trembling hand on my thigh as he took me into his mouth. In that moment, all that I had worked so hard for, trying to be normal by imagining the faceless girls, shattered into a mind-blowing orgasm that left me shaken and riddled with guilt.

"Brian, darlin', are you all right?" Jamie's mother, Patsy Mayfield, asked quietly, breaking into my thoughts as she passed the collection plate down our row. Tossing in the few dollars that Carolyn had given to me, I wiped my hand across my forehead, brushing my damp brown curls out of my eyes. I was sweating, and my skin was clammy. She, however, looked perfectly at ease, even in the light sweater covering her blinding yellow sundress. A single braid held her long blond hair back down her back. It was obvious where Jamie had gotten his beautiful hair and delicate features. Her hazel eyes were the only difference, because his were like sapphires. But her eyes were also kind as she watched me with concern.

"No, ma'am, I'm sorry. I don't feel well," I told her, looking up slowly, my hopeful brown eyes meeting hers. It was true; I didn't feel well, not at all. The guilt brought on by the sermon was causing my stomach to lurch precariously, having just found out that I was going to burn in hell for something I absolutely could not control. I'd tried to control it, but my wiring was all wrong. I wanted to have sex with boys, and I was surely going to spend eternity in the lake of fire because of it. That was certain to cause some measure of nausea.

"Well, the service is just about over. Why don't you leave a little early and head home? I'm glad you could stay over and go to church with us this morning. I'd love to see you attend more regularly," she whispered as the murmuring died down. Her voice was soft and kind, like you would expect any mother's voice to be. Then, with a reassuring smile, she added, "I told you maybe cold pizza for breakfast wasn't a good idea," and patted my hand.

I tried to smile back, but it just came off feeling more like a grimace. Before Jamie or anyone else could call me back, I walked swiftly for the double doors. The disapproving faces flashed past me, row after row, making me feel like a criminal escaping from prison. At any moment, one of them could try to stop me, could call me back to finish my Sunday morning sentence. Once I pushed through the left door at the back of the small church, I broke into a sprint, and I did not stop until I had reached my own back porch.

Sprinting through the humid, ninety-degree heat, it was a wonder I hadn't collapsed. I'd balled up my too-tight suit jacket and wrapped my tie around the other hand as I climbed up the stairs. The cluttered screened-in porch offered a small respite for me to catch my breath. I took off my shoes, as was customary at my foster parents' home, and leaned on the arm of the yellowing wicker sofa that dominated the space. I couldn't remember what color the cushions on the worn-out couch had been originally, but now it held a faded jungle print, washed out by years of the sun's harsh rays.

The Schreibers, my foster parents of nearly five years, were the best I'd ever had. They had little money because Dr. Schreiber was on staff at the local hospital and not in private practice. What they lacked in financial strength, they made up for with an abundance of stability and compassion. One junkie looking for a stereo to hock for drugs had changed the course of my life, but I felt safer here than any home that I'd lived in since my parents died. I had only been three years old, so I remembered little about them now, just flashes, vague impressions, and half-forgotten nightmares.

I tried to open the door quietly, but luck was just not on my side. Carolyn was standing in the kitchen, and I watched her for a moment as she pulled a fresh apple pie from the oven. To be honest, I was thankful for her and for her husband, Richard. Reluctant as I was to admit it, I felt rather ashamed of my first thoughts of my foster father. Richard had specifically requested a teenage boy to be placed with them. At first I thought he was one of those. I had already dealt with a few of them in foster care.

One such foster parent was Mrs. Butler, who would come into my room at night and make me jack off while she watched. I was eleven years old, so I did not know about the context or the scope of the act, only the quick breathless instructions she had given me that first time. She got so excited when I would finally blow. I remember her face would get all red, and she'd kind of bounce a little in the chair she sat in next to my bed. It took forever, because it was hard to get all worked up with your foster mom watching you get off. Even though she would always try to "help me clean up," I'd just grab the towel from her and get under the covers, terrified that one night she would want to get in bed with me. To be honest, she fucking creeped me out. However, it wasn't long before Child Services removed me from her care and placed with the Schreibers because they had been called to investigate the rumor that Mrs. Butler was having sex with my younger foster brother. Only eight. He wasn't old enough or strong enough to resist her. I was thankful that I had never seen her again.

Richard was different, though. He just wanted a teenage boy because in his sixties, he was getting too old to do certain chores around the house and needed some help. Richard and Carolyn had taken in foster kids years ago, after their baby boy had suddenly died in his crib. The southern wall of the living room contained a dutifully maintained a montage of school pictures from each of their charges. At eleven, about to turn twelve, I had been the closest they could find to what they wanted, but he seemed happy enough with me.

"You're home early," Carolyn commented as she turned off the oven. Shrugging, I looked away from her gaze, noticing the mess on the kitchen counter. She was a fantastic cook, but her cleaning skills left something to be desired. Tossing my balled-up jacket and tie onto one of the kitchen chairs, I went over to the counter. Feeling a little calmer now that I was out from under the preacher's watchful eye, I cleared away some of the mess. After a few moments, I felt Carolyn's hand on my shoulder.

"Is everything okay, Brian?" she asked gently. This was exactly why I didn't mind helping around the house—cleaning the gutters, mowing the yard, and doing dishes. She was the closest thing I could ever remember having for a mother. Because I was just a toddler when my parents died, I only have a vague memory of my mother, a memory somewhere between Sesame Street and potty training. I briefly considered talking to her about how I felt, but since I wasn't really sure about her views, I just couldn't take the chance. Reaching behind her, she untied the worn apron and hung it on a peg behind the door. Pushing her graying, light-brown hair back in the general area of her messy bun, she watched me with speculative concern, but I remained silent, concentrating on my cleaning. She took off her oval-rimmed glasses to rub her deep-set gray eyes.

"Going to hell, are we, Brian McAllister?" she finally asked in an offhand voice. Spinning where I stood, I openly gaped at her, the cluttered counter forgotten in an instant. In my shock, I couldn't even form the words to find out why she would ask me that. "Old Preacher Moore thinks everyone is going to hell for one thing or another. Whether it's Richard for having wine with supper or me for gossipin' with the ladies in my sewing circle, someone's always in trouble," she said with a chuckle. "I'm sure whatever you're feeling all guilty about isn't worth fussin' over. You're a good kid, Brian."

"Thanks, Carolyn," I told her with genuine affection, though not altogether reassured, and turned back to cleaning. She couldn't know that I had nothing to worry about, since she didn't know how I felt or what I'd done. For all I knew, she may agree with the preacher about boys being attracted to other boys. After wiping down the counter, dodging the obstacle course of appliances, racks, and the newly baked pie, I dropped the rag on the divider between the two sides of the stainless steel sink and grabbed the broom from the corner. As I swept the flour from the worn pattern on the slightly warped tile floor, she continued to talk.

"Now, if it has anything to do with the...," she started and then lowered her voice to a whisper, "birds and the bees...." She looked meaningfully at me and then resumed in her normal tone, "talk to Richard. The last thing on earth you need in your already tough life is to knock up some cheerleader."

I almost laughed right out loud at that. *If only*, I thought wryly, but just nodded, and finally the thoroughly awkward subject was closed.

That night, after cleaning up the supper dishes, I lay in my bed and stared up at the blank expanse of ceiling over my head for a long time. Not for the first time, under the guise of attempting sleep, my eyes traced its cracks and imperfections. My bedroom was simple, but safe and warm, which was exactly what I needed. The small student desk under the window was perfect for doing schoolwork or building models whenever I got them for Christmas or birthdays. That was my passion, building things. I had built ships and cars from kits, but lately I had been working on buildings with old scraps of trash that I had found around the house—toilet paper and paper towel rolls, newspaper, and for signs I would use color advertisements from magazines. It was wonderful of Richard and Carolyn to indulge me in my fascination with models when they could.

The dresser, with its deep scratches and gouge marks, held my finished models and my clothes, and looked like it literally had fallen off the back of a truck. The bed was a slightly different story. After years of housing a couple of foster kids at a time, they had gotten too old to handle the discipline problems that usually accompanied abandoned and sometimes abused children. So, after their last two charges had turned eighteen, they'd decided to only have one at a time and had replaced their bunk beds with one brand new sturdy twin. It was the most comfortable bed I'd ever had. The worn green comforter, good no matter the gender of the kid sleeping in the bed, was warm and reassuring. I couldn't have asked for anything better.

My thoughts raced as I continued to trace the cracks in the ceiling with my tired eyes. I thought about what Carolyn had said; *maybe I wasn't so horrible after all. I mean, I didn't want to be like this; I didn't want to like boys. Maybe there was something wrong with me that a doctor could help with. Maybe I should talk to Richard.* A small measure of hope flared within me at that thought. *Or maybe that was the way God intended for me to be? If He had absolute control over everyone and everything, why would he have made me bad? Broken? Wrong?*

It was hours before sleep finally took me.

"Hey man, are you feeling any better?" Jamie asked as I slammed my locker closed with a rather loud bang. As he leaned casually against the wall nearby, I noticed that his lanky body had become more defined under the jeans and soft blue T-shirt he wore. That shirt was my favorite on him.

Slowly raising my eyes to his face, I wondered if he could see right through me. His furrowed brow made him look worried. That made me conflicted because I loved that he cared, even if it was only as a friend, but I felt guilty about my attraction to him, my need for him. I was terrified that someone would find out about that need, because our small town ostracized anyone who was even the least bit different from the stereotypical Southern boy. Vilified them and anyone close to them. I couldn't imagine that Carolyn would appreciate being asked to leave her sewing circle because of her queer foster kid.

"I'm fine," I told him in a clipped tone, not meeting his eyes. "Let's go to class." When I moved to walk around him, but he grabbed my arm. A feeling like an electric current shot through my skin, and I pulled away sharply. When my eyes finally met his, the hurt and confusion I saw in them tore at me. Pushing past him gently, not wanting to make either of us feel more uncomfortable, I headed for English. Jamie was right behind me as we passed door after door of teenagers piling into their classes. Out of the corner of my eye, I saw a couple of people wave at Jamie, but he only gave them a halfhearted nod. His legs were longer, so he had caught up with me by the time we reached the doorway to our first class. He said nothing, just took his customary seat to the right of mine.

I felt like people were staring at me, the hairs on the back of my neck standing on end. Glancing around, I saw that the rest of the kids in the room were only now taking out their books, getting ready for class to start. Feeling utterly paranoid, I turned back around in my seat and noticed Jamie watching me surreptitiously from my right. Grabbing my English book, a beat-up notebook, and my pen, I turned and waited not-so-patiently for the teacher. I was about to pay strict attention in class for probably the first time that year.

For the next hour, I earnestly tried to pay attention to the material being presented, nearly boring a hole in the wall behind Mrs. Cornell's head with my unflinching stare. By the time the bell rang, I could have told you how many books were in the bookcase behind her desk, listed every piece of paper on the bulletin board, and described the intricate pattern of the crack in her "Best Teacher Ever" coffee mug. Doing everything I could to push the fear out of my mind was fruitless, however, because of all the sideways glances from Jamie. He must have tried to catch my eye at least thirty times during the hour-long lesson, and if he didn't fucking stop, people were going to talk. Nothing in the world caused more drama than teenagers. *What if people suspected? What if they started rumors about us? What would I do then?*

We spent the rest of the day in a similar manner. Our school was small, so the whole, entire junior class moved as one from room to room, trudging down the hall together like a chain gang of criminals out for their afternoon at the rock quarry. Some people ventured off to band instead of choir, or remedial math instead of algebra, but Jamie was a constant throughout my day.

At that point, it was both a blessing and a curse.

The thought of sitting next to him, trying to ignore the gnawing guilt in my stomach for the entire lunch hour, was not pleasant. When the bell rang signaling lunch, I told him I had to get my lunch bag from my locker and I'd meet him in the cafeteria. Of course, there was no bag. I headed past the hallway that led to my locker and kept walking right through the double doors and outside. Sitting on the far side of a large oak, away from the few students who had ventured out on the gloomy day, I noticed it looked like a storm was threatening, but I didn't care. Let the skies open up and wash away my sins.

As I sat outside, away from the watchful eyes of several dozen nosy teenagers and away from Jamie's baleful stares, I could relax a little and breathe again. The panic returned when I thought of having to hide like this for the next six weeks until school was out. *It was only the end of April now; how the hell was I supposed to keep this up until the beginning of June?* If someone started the rumor, or even just insinuated that I spent just a little too much time tagging along after Jamie Mayfield, it could ruin us both. The fear settled in my stomach, rooting itself there, like an infestation of my body and soul.

Our last class of the day was the generic rotating "extra" electives. That day, it was art. Music was actually my favorite extra elective class, but art wasn't bad. I enjoyed the creative element, and usually it was a pleasant diversion from the normal boredom that made up our high school curriculum. As Jamie and I walked in, we saw Mr. Barnes in the back of the room, setting out supplies. He wore a similar T-shirt, sweater vest, and khakis to the ones I'd seen him in every Monday since the start of the term. It almost screamed "gay," but I mean, everyone in school knew that already; it wasn't like you couldn't tell.

I stopped dead in the doorway, Jamie nearly slamming into me from behind. Mr. Barnes was gay. Everyone knew Mr. Barnes was gay; he just gave off that vibe. *Would everyone know about me?* I'd never really given it any thought before. Like the pea-green walls of the art room, it had just become like background noise. *What if he could tell that I thought about other guys?* Suddenly, I felt sick and fell onto the bench at the picnic-like table, my skin crawling with a cold sweat.

Ignoring Jamie completely, I rushed through my charcoal representation of a birdhouse and was cleaning up long before the bell rang. For the remaining twenty minutes of class, feeling Jamie's worried gaze as he worked, I stared unseeingly out of the classroom window, trying to figure out what the hell I was going to do. When class ended, Jamie looked at me once and then left the room without another word.

I had a feeling I would have to get used to that. It did nothing to help the sick feeling in my stomach.

"Brian? Could you stick around for a minute?" Mr. Barnes requested quietly as everyone else filed out of the room and into the hall. I looked around wildly at the slowly emptying wooden tables with loose benches, but I didn't see anyone looking or whispering. No one seemed surprised or even interested in his request. I had to get a hold of myself, or I would be the one to expose my secret.

Packing up my stuff, I tried to look like everyone else, but I felt trapped, panicky. Once the rest of the class had left the room, I sat back down at the art bench. My breathing was shallow and uneven as I used my nail to pick at a spot of dried paint. Not even having the balls to look him in the eye, I just sat there, waiting for the axe to fall. *He knew. He had to know, or why else would he want to talk to me?* I'd never been in trouble, never been disrespectful. I felt sick that now everyone else would know, too. My life would be over. Maybe the Schreibers would even send me back to the State. I mean, who wanted a perverted freak in the next bedroom?

"Brian, I've noticed that you have been fairly distracted the last few classes. You seem upset about something," he started, sitting down across from me. He folded his arms delicately on the worn and scored wooden table. I could feel his eyes on my face. "Is everything all right at home?"

"Yeah," I said quietly, only it came out more like a croak than an actual word. *Why was he dragging this out? Couldn't he just get on with it? My life was going to be ruined now; didn't he have the decency to make my end swift?* It was like he was trying to perform surgery with a dull, rusty scalpel.

"Brian, unless someone is physically hurting you, which I don't think is the case, anything that you tell me will stay between us," he reassured gently. Finally, I raised my head.

"It's not... No one is hurting me," I started hesitantly. "I just... I can't talk about it." I really wanted to talk to someone, anyone who could help me not feel so fucking scared all the time. But I was afraid that once I said it out loud, it would be true. It would be real. I would be gay, and everyone would know. My friends, the other kids at school, the Schreibers... Jamie. They would all know.

"Does it have anything to do with Jamie Mayfield?" My eyes shot up to meet his solemn eyes; his normally impassive face had softened. "I noticed that you two were distant today. Usually you're two peas in a pod," he mused, and I blanched. *If he had noticed what Jamie meant to me, would other people notice too, or was it just because he was gay?* I couldn't drag Jamie down with me in this. His parents were such zealots about their religion, they would never forgive him. Shaking my head violently, I tried to quell the panic rolling in my stomach.

"I know I'm a teacher, but I might just understand," he offered, patting my arm as he stood. "If you change your mind, my door is always open. Please, come and see me anytime, okay?" Nodding as I grabbed my bag, I practically ran from the room. I had debated about just telling him, just saying the words. All I had to say was that I thought I might be gay, but the fear of saying it out loud, making it tangible, pushed me out the door without looking back.

For the rest of the week, I did my best to appear normal. I went to all of my classes, spent time in the cafeteria at lunch, and tried to be engaged in conversations with our friends. The last thing I wanted was for anyone to suspect that there was something bothering me—or more to the point, something wrong with me. I'd been scared of how I felt for years, but now that my feelings for Jamie had been more clearly defined and labeled as evil, it was all I could think about. Only Jamie had really figured out that I was having some kind of problem. I caught him watching me a few times—in class, at lunch with our friends, and at our lockers. I had made a point of not being alone with him. If we weren't alone, he couldn't corner me to ask what was wrong. I knew I wouldn't be able to keep it up forever, but it was all going fairly smoothly—until Friday afternoon.

Gym had never been my favorite class, but I tolerated it because it wasn't exactly optional. I didn't mind the physical exertion or the games that we played; it was the drill sergeant they called a teacher. Coach Williams was recently back from his overseas deployment and worked us like we were storming the beaches at Normandy rather than just trying to earn high school credit. However, lately the gym had become almost physical torture. Being in the showers, naked near Jamie, it was all I could do to think of baseball stats and multiplication tables to stop myself from getting hard. I had to force myself not to watch as he used his bare hands to lather up his skin. Those were images to feed the fantasies I would have later at night as I lay alone in bed.

Friday, however, I had one more factor working against me. In my quest to become more normal, I hadn't masturbated all week. If I didn't masturbate, I couldn't think of guys while doing it. If I thought about sex at all, the next thing that popped into my mind was that stout preacher man. That was a wonderful way to kill my libido. In my imagination, he was standing there, using his huge ham-like hands to push me straight to hell to atone for my sins.

Only right then, it wasn't working.

Unfortunately, without that release, I was paying for my pent-up sexual tension. I hadn't even taken off my gym uniform of short shorts and tight T-shirt emblazoned with our red and white school colors, and I was already hard. I knew there was no way I could strip and get into the showers. Completely mortified, I stood in the boys' locker room, surrounded by thirty of my half-naked male classmates. Looking over in alarm, I noticed Jamie watching me. My locker was open in front of me, the door blocking my bulging shorts, but I had to get out of there. I couldn't let him or anyone else see the sight of other naked boys aroused me. After throwing the jeans and T-shirt I had worn to school into my backpack, I ran, not really having any kind of plan where I would end up.

I had sprinted about a block from the high school when I realized it was raining, but my momentum and my adrenaline continued to carry me forward, anyway. I ran through the streets and past the quiet houses until finally I stopped at a garage overhang where I could catch my breath out of the rain. Bent over with my hands on my knees, I gulped down air. Extremely pleased that my erection had finally gone down, I remained partially stooped, panting. The mist dripping off the roof cooled the back of my neck as I tried to get myself under control. The noise of the driving rain on the tin roof over my head masked the sound of heavy footsteps pounding toward the garage. I didn't have any sign that Jamie was approaching until he stood in front of me. When I tried to make a break for it, he grabbed my shirt.

"Fuck no," he said in a stern voice, and I gaped at him. I don't think I had ever heard him swear before. "You and I are going to go to my house to talk—now." I looked away from the alley. With a sinking feeling, I realized we stood just yards from his house. Without even thinking about it, I had run right to him, or at least to his home. He dragged me the few remaining feet to his back gate, and, resigned to my fate, I let him push me through it.

Seeing the house that held so many wonderful memories for me, I felt my insides go cold. *What the hell was I going to tell him? I couldn't tell him the truth.* As we climbed up the stairs of the large wooden deck, I knew I wouldn't be able to lie to him. He was the best friend I had ever had, and deep down, I cared for him much more than I should have. The rain spattered against the large bay windows that overlooked the Mayfield's kitchen. The white trim around the window seemed to set off the light-gray siding perfectly. Everything about Jamie's house, from the expensive brick patio to the perfectly cut lawn, said "upper middle class." It was just another reason Jamie and I could never be more than what we were. His parents tolerated me as the local charity case; they would never accept me as anything more.

When we got to the back door, he swore again. I turned to look at him and, for the first time, noticed that he was still wearing his gym uniform. He must have taken off right after me. The white and red T-shirt clung to his chest, and while I didn't check, I was sure the shorts were clinging as well.

"I left my fucking keys at school." He looked around, and I saw his eyes fix on the tree house. We had spent so many hours in it when we were younger. It was one of the first places I had ever felt safe after coming to live with the Schreibers. I had mostly forgotten about it now that we were in high school. At nearly seventeen, we were a little old to be playing in tree houses. In fact, I think Jamie had said his dad was going to take it down at the end of the summer.

I still remembered how completely impressed I'd been the first time I had seen it. Jamie's father masterfully built it from sturdy pine with a real roof like that on their home. Apparently, Jamie's father had built it around the time they'd had their roof redone, and he'd used the leftover material to build a roof for the tree house. The wood looked old and a little rough, and there were large openings on two sides with shutters tied closed to keep out the elements. The whole tree house looked battered now. Even the wooden ladder, which was simply the front part of a painter's ladder disassembled and affixed to the gigantic oak, was showing signs of wear.

The model of the tree house sitting on my dresser was in much better condition.

Climbing up the old ladder and pushing through the trapdoor at the top, we stood hunched in the small space, which seemed to have shrunk since the last time I had been up there. A six-foot-by-six-foot space seems so much larger when you're just a kid. The pictures of different comic book heroes that we had drawn as kids still hung on the walls. Most of the paper was molded and yellowed with age, the tape that held them up peeling and brittle. The bean bag chairs that Mrs. Mayfield had made for us were long gone, but the milk crates and scrap wood we'd used for a table were still there. Playing cards and various broken crayons were strewn over the table and floor.

Sitting down in the corner, I brushed a cobweb from the ceiling just above my head as Jamie shrugged out of his wet T-shirt and hung it on a nearby nail. The sight of him, so close and shirtless, made my temperature jump in our impromptu confessional. It was already hot and musty in the closed space, but his proximity intensified that, and I felt the sweat bead on my forehead and cheeks. He sat down on the floor, cross-legged, right in front of me, and stared into my face for a long moment. Then he spoke.

"What did I do?" His voice was tender but strong, as though determined to get an answer. "Please, just tell me what I did." The pain in his eyes was heartbreaking to me. I couldn't believe he thought I was mad at him, that he had done something wrong. But looking back at my behavior over the last week, I could understand how he might have come to that conclusion. Stunting our conversations, avoiding him, running from him in the gym—yeah, I certainly followed his logic.

I had to tell him.

I couldn't tell him.

He would hate me, and I would lose my best friend.

That thought was like a knife through my heart, and I felt my throat burn. *Oh God, I couldn't cry in front of him too, not after everything else that had happened today.* He already had to think I was a pansy. Looking up at the ceiling, I tried desperately to calm myself, but it was no use. The tears fell.

"Brian, please," he murmured and scooted closer. Then his arm was around my shoulders and I pressed my forehead against his neck. He was holding me, and it felt so fucking good. This wasn't like the quick hug I'd given him when his aunt had died last year, or even the tight squeeze he'd given me last week when I'd thought I was going to fail my math test. The way he was holding me, comforting me, was something else entirely, and it felt so fucking good to not feel like a freak, even if only for just a few minutes. He pressed his template against my shoulder, and I could feel his quick breath against my wet skin. It was like every dream I'd ever had about being with him, only better because he was actually here, touching me. Jamie's touch felt so tender that I could pretend for that one moment we were everything I had wanted us to be. Before I could sink too far into my fantasy, I pulled away, but slowly, hesitantly, he turned his face to the side and kissed the exposed skin of my neck. I sucked in a breath, stunned. The feeling of his soft lips on my throat, even just in that small comforting gesture, shocked me into complete and utter silence. I did not know what to say, no idea what to do next. All I knew was, in that moment, I needed to look into his eyes. I had to know what he felt.

When I pulled back, I saw the shock and utter terror that I was feeling reflected at me from his perfect face.

CHAPTER TWO

As I watched, his expression softened, the fear and the shock replaced by a different emotion. He kept his eyes on mine and leaned forward ever so slightly, and then hesitated. If I hadn't been watching him so intently, I wouldn't have noticed that he had moved at all. When I didn't punch, scream, or even back away, he leaned in a little closer—an unspoken question in his eyes.

Do you feel it too?

I felt his warm breath on my face; he was so damn close. My heart rate sped up wildly, and I could hear the blood pounding in my ears. He whispered, almost too softly for me to hear.

"Please... please don't hate me."

Then, in the lightest of touches, soft but unyielding, his lips pressed against mine. My eyes closed, and I felt a rush of emotion, sexual tension, something building within me. As his mouth molded over the contours of my lips, we reveled in the untamed surge of passion that flowed between us. The kiss was delicate, sweet, and lingered just long enough to make me want more. I had waited my whole life for my first kiss, and while it wasn't exactly how I'd pictured it in my youth, it was perfect. His lips were warm and smooth as they moved against mine, causing a swelling tension in my stomach. The rain continued to pound the tree house roof as my arms nearly ached to go around him, but I didn't want to break the spell that had enveloped us. It was everything that a boy's first kiss should be.

Only it wasn't with a girl.

He pulled back slowly, almost reluctantly, probably waiting for me to bolt or call him names. When I did neither, his face broke into a shy smile and he ran one hand through his unruly, damp hair. The other was still to the side of my legs, using it to prop himself up with a forced casual air. We were so close that his body heat radiated against my skin. Still trembling from fear or excitement, I was too shocked to move. This was absolutely surreal, like my fantasies had all come true in an instant. I really thought that humans would land on Mars before Jamie and I would be kissing. It thrilled and terrified me.

Where the hell did we go from there?

It was also the best and the worst thing that could have happened.

He couldn't feel the same way about me I felt about him, could he?

"I have wanted to do that for such a long time," he whispered, leaning back on his palms, his legs remaining crossed in front of him as he sat facing me. I continued to lean back against the wall of our sanctuary. His body heat against my cool, damp skin made me shiver. Or maybe it was his proximity. I just sat watching him. Somehow, incredibly, I knew he was the same person he had been that morning, but it seemed like the whole dynamic of our relationship had shifted with that one kiss. I suddenly felt shy, almost awkward, with him.

"I didn't know," I said, looking down at my hands, and then added, "I thought it was just me." His sharp intake of breath caused me to look up, and I watched as his face brightened briefly into a radiant smile. My heart swelled, and in that moment, the only thing that existed was him. *He didn't hate me. He didn't think I was some sick, perverted freak. He felt the same way I did. But what would we do?*

"I thought I was an abomination," I murmured under my breath.

"Is that why you've been so upset? Because of what the preacher said in church last Sunday?" As I nodded, he ran his hand through his damp hair again. It was a nervous gesture, something he did when he had a lot on his mind. "If I'd known, I would have told Mama that you were sick so you wouldn't have had to go. I hate his sermon upset you."

Taking a deep breath, I tried searching his face for answers. I had no other choice but to talk to him about how I felt about him, and I didn't know where the conversation might lead. For the first time since we'd met, a fresh set of possibilities opened for us. The conversation was going to be harder because I didn't know how to frame the question I wanted to ask him. To be honest, I wasn't even sure I wanted to hear his answer. I wasn't a very religious person, and the Schreibers weren't church people. I didn't have the frame of reference I needed to interpret the sermon. Mrs. Mayfield thought everyone should go every Sunday, and by dragging me along when I stayed over, she felt like she was helping to save my soul. Jamie, however, had been attending his entire life. Pastor Moore had even baptized him in that church as a baby. Surely, Jamie was more of an expert on religion and God than I was.

"Do you think he's right?" I asked Jamie in almost a whisper, averting my gaze to focus on a knot in the old floorboard, suddenly unable to look him in the eye. "Are we... Is it... is it wrong, the way I feel about you?"

He turned and crawled to sit next to me; tossing a broken action figure out of his way before leaning back against the wall. We were side by side, his arm brushing mine casually, my breath catching in my throat at the light contact. I leaned toward him, resting my head on his shoulder. It was strange that the gesture felt so natural to me. Just an hour before, the thought of showing this kind of affection for him had terrified me. As it was, my heart rate sped because again, he was so close.

"I don't know, Brian," he whispered again, so softly into my hair that he was almost afraid to say it out loud. His breath caused an eruption of goose bumps on my cold, damp skin. "I can't believe that how I feel about you is wrong. Just being with you like this, knowing that I'm not alone, it's the happiest I've been in a long time. I don't know how that can be wrong. But the Bible references that the preacher used seemed pretty clear. My question is, if God hates gay people and God made us, why would He make people He hated? I thought God was supposed to love everybody? Is this a test? Why me? Why you?" I sat there, contemplating his questions. My own questions were exactly the same. I wondered if maybe other boys had those same difficulties.

Then, the feeling that had been churning inside me for weeks, the one that had intensified to a fever pitch in the last week, came screaming to the surface.

"I'm scared, Jamie," I admitted quietly, finally voicing my fear for the first time. Turning his head slightly, he kissed my hair. He was only a few months older than me; he'd already turned seventeen while I was still sixteen. But at that moment, he made me feel safe. He made me feel like the rest of it, the preacher, the hatred, even the word gay—none of it mattered. Feeling safe wasn't something that I was used to, so I held on to that feeling for as long as I could.

"Me too," he whispered back after a moment, wrapping his hand around mine, squeezing it tightly where it lay on my thigh. He meant to comfort me, but that one gesture, so intimate, made our situation that much more real to me. A kiss was one thing, but holding my hand, like we were a couple, was too much for me. No matter how much I had wanted him, wanted to be comforted by him, I had never entertained the possibility that it could ever really happen. My attraction to him had just been a sick, dark fantasy that I had been trying to push out of my head for a long time. Suddenly, it had all become real.

We were going to go to hell and God would exile us if our relationship progressed any further. I couldn't let that happen—not to him. Jamie was a good and loving person. If anyone deserved to go to heaven when they died, it was him. Suddenly, I had to know if what the preacher said was true or if it was his own warped interpretation. If he were wrong, Jamie and I would be free to be together without fear of damnation. There had to be rules he had to follow; he must have gone to school. *Wouldn't someone know if he wasn't being truthful?*

"I should get home," I said, standing abruptly, and his face filled with hurt, and his eyes remained downcast briefly before he recovered. He thought I was pulling away from him; he had shared this epic moment with me, and he thought I was going to walk away from him. "Jamie, I just need time to think because I never dreamed that you—"

"No, I get it, Brian, really," he cut me off mid-sentence as he stood. I tried not to watch the small bead of sweat rolling down his pale chest as he swiped the wet dust and dirt from the back of his gym shorts. He was going to have to wash those once he got inside, or his mama was going to have a fit. "I know this is a lot to take in. I think we both have some things to think about."

It broke me to see that look on his face, lost and defeated. Taking a few calming breaths, I closed my eyes. Then, summoning up every bit of courage that I had, I put my hand on his face, stroking his cheek with my thumb. He looked at me curiously, and on an impulse, I wrapped my arms around his neck and pulled him to me. Tilting my head slightly, I pressed my lips to his once more. Even though the rain was pounding the roof of the tree house, I distinctly heard him moan into the kiss. I kept my hips away from him so that he wouldn't feel the growing erection in my gym shorts.

This kiss had a slight twinge of hunger, of desperation, to it. Our teeth knocked together a few times in our need to be closer. I cocked my head to the other side, pressing my upper body harder against him, deepening the kiss even further. My mouth opened, and our tongues touched lightly, hesitantly, almost as if we were both scared of it happening. The feeling of his warm, naked skin under my hands drove most of the reason from me, but eventually I pulled away. When we broke apart, we were both panting. I heard his long, inaudible sigh of the word "wow," and I chuckled quietly before turning for the trapdoor.

I arrived home to an empty house about ten minutes later, and I was thankful. It wasn't terribly unusual, since Richard kept regular hours at the hospital and Carolyn had her various causes. She volunteered, reading to the kids at the local elementary school, and sometimes worked at the senior center. She also ran errands during the day, so I couldn't even guess where she'd be right now. I went to my room and stripped out of my wet gym uniform, tossing it into the nearby hamper. Later tonight, I would have to do a load of laundry; I usually did my laundry anyway, so it wouldn't be out of the ordinary, but I didn't need Carolyn running across my wet gym uniform caked with dirt. Standing there, alone in the confines of my room, naked, letting the gentle breeze from the open window wash over me, I felt a flare of pure sexual need race through me. I got hard, my pulse quickening as I thought about the kiss that Jamie and I had just shared. I had work to do, however, so I picked up the towel I had grabbed from the linen closet and dried myself off.

Dressing in boxers and a loose pair of shorts, I skipped socks or even a shirt because of the heat. The rain had cooled things off some, but not nearly enough; it was still sweltering in the house. As I headed down the hall to Richard's office, I wondered if I would find any answers, if anyone had insight into my confusion. *Surely people would put that kind of information on the Internet? Could I find anything to justify the attraction that Jamie and I felt for each other? What if all I found was the hellfire and damnation that the preacher warned us of? Could I give Jamie up? Could I force myself into the life that God apparently wanted me to lead? Could I live that kind of lie?*

Richard's office wasn't the opulent space that you would expect a doctor to have in his home. He wasn't pretentious like that, but it was clean, comfortable, and functional. I looked around at the simply decorated office with its farmland prints and fake silk flowers and decided that this was better. It was more inviting than the magazine layout-like offices that most doctors would have. Richard had never discouraged me from coming into his office, but he'd never exactly encouraged it either, so I felt nervous just being in there. However, it wasn't the research I could do in the school library. I was sure that the school's computers had something that tracked where we went on the Internet, and I couldn't guarantee that I would ever be alone to search.

Richard would never have to know.

My palms were sweaty when I sat down in his worn leather chair, jumping slightly when I bumped the desk with my knee and the desktop appeared. Grabbing the mouse, I moved it around the desktop, looking for the Internet browser. I wasn't a computer whiz, but I hoped that a quick Internet search would give me what I needed. Maybe other people had the same questions that Jamie and I had. Better yet, maybe someone had answers to those questions.

Peeking out the window to make sure Carolyn's car wasn't in the drive, I brought up the Internet browser. I felt like a criminal as I clicked in the address bar, looked over my shoulder, and typed in the address for a search engine. *But what to search for? What did the preacher hate the most?* I typed in "gay men" and hit enter. The screen nearly exploded with responses—over fifty-two million of them. I clicked on the first one, absently checking over my shoulder again. I knew there was no one there, but my guilty conscience made me feel like someone was watching. When I turned back to the screen, I couldn't find the close button fast enough. From every corner of the screen, naked boys and naked men smiled at me from various positions and assorted stages of sex. I clicked the minimize button, paranoid that someone would see it from the second-story window.

I opened another window and went back to the search engine to try something else. That time I typed in "+gay +God," and got considerably fewer results. Well, thirty-eight million was considerably fewer, but it was still a large number. I scrolled through the results this time and found a lot of information. From the kid whose parents sent him to a homosexual rehabilitation center in California and no

one ever heard from him again, to the hellfire and damnation that I
expected, to the fight against allowing gay people to get married. It
wasn't until the third page that I found a site asking why God made
people gay. Intrigued, I clicked on it. It was a letter that a pastor had
written to one of his congregants about the boy being gay. At first, the
reverend believed that the boy would indeed go to hell, but after he
researched the matter using his Bible and other religious and secular
resources, he came to a much different conclusion.

He felt that how people understand the Bible stemmed from their
background. For example, if your father believed that homosexuality
was wrong and taught that to you your entire life, you would interpret
the Bible similarly because someone taught it to you. To me, this meant
that ten different people could read those same passages that Preacher
Moore had and come up with ten different meanings from them. Some
would agree with how he understood it, and some wouldn't. The site
talked about how this man of God interpreted the Bible on the topic
of homosexuality. The story of creation, the story of Sodom, and even
the same passages from Romans that Pastor Moore had used took on a
whole different meaning for him.

So, another religious source believed we weren't going to hell. That
gave me hope. *If scholars and religious men couldn't agree on the subject,
it meant the answer wasn't definitive.* That one insignificant detail made
me feel better. Again, I checked out the window to make sure I was
still alone before clicking the print button and printing the long
explanation for Jamie, because I wasn't sure if I could relay all the
information accurately enough or answer questions that he might have
on it. I wanted him to see the article for himself. Watching the paper
come slowly out of the printer, I had to admit, even just to myself, a
sense of relief. After the dozen sheets printed, I grabbed them from the

tray and clicked the close button on the browser. It was only then that I remembered the other window that was open. Sneaking yet another glance around and out the window, I reopened the browser, allowing myself to look at it again. I felt embarrassed and guilty about looking at it, but I was curious.

That one flash of the screen I had seen before I minimized it made me really fucking excited. I looked over at each of the couples until my eyes focused on one pair. One boy was lying on his back, his head thrown back in obvious pleasure, while the other boy, a blonde, performed oral sex on him. It wasn't the act that caught my attention; it was the blonde. He was beautiful.

Just then, the wind rustled through the leaves of the enormous maple tree next to the window. I checked guiltily over my shoulder again before turning my attention back to the blonde on the screen. He was beautiful because he reminded me of Jamie. It was like watching Jamie give head. It made me hard just to think about it.

I shut down the computer quickly and, chancing another glance out the window, then walked to my room with tented shorts. When I closed the door behind me with those wild, decadent images burned into my mind. Only in my head, it was me on my back and Jamie was on his knees over me. Taking the printed papers, I hid them under a shoebox on my closet shelf, even though no one ever went into my closet since I did my laundry. I didn't want anyone coming across them by accident. Grabbing the towel I had used to dry off earlier, I walked over to my bed. Then I checked the window next to my bed, which also overlooked the drive, and saw it was still empty. I pulled the covers back, and after doubling the towel, spread it on the bed.

I had masturbated countless times over the last few years, and I had always forced myself to think about girls to pigeonhole myself into the mold I thought I belonged in. This time, I wanted to think about Jamie. Though I couldn't imagine why he wanted a scrawny, mousey-haired boy like me, average in every way, right down to a mild case of acne. The only thing about my appearance that I really liked was my curly hair. Having let it grow out over the last few years, I noticed the resemblance to my mother much more clearly now. That single piece of paper that I had carried with me from place to place and house to house was the only picture I had of my parents. When I was about eight, one of my older foster siblings, one of the few nice ones, had helped me find the news article on the computer, the one that described my parents' deaths. We had printed it quietly, in the dead of night, after everyone had gone to bed.

I pulled off my shorts and boxers, feeling more naked than I ever had, and lay down on the towel. Every time I had done this before, I had always just pulled my sleep pants down over my hips and pulled them right up afterwards because I felt ashamed. However, this time I didn't feel ashamed as I thought about Jamie's kiss from earlier that afternoon, sweet and full of promise. I ran my fingers over my lips, remembering the perfect feeling of his lips on mine. My erection was throbbing as I moved my fingers down over my chest. That was something I had not done previously; I hadn't thought that I should take such delight in the act. Masturbation was just something that needed to be done, not something to revel in. My hips rolled as my nipples hardened, the light caress of my fingers causing my skin to tingle. I couldn't stop the low moan that came from deep in my chest as my head pressed back against the pillow and my hips bucked uselessly up into empty space.

As my back arched, my bottom pressed hard into the mattress and my fingers traced a slow line across my flat stomach. I spread my legs wider as my right hand encircled my erection and my left trailed farther down between my legs. My hard cock pulsed in my hand as I rubbed my scrotum and thighs. I pictured that image of the two boys in my head, only they turned into Jamie and me. He looked down at me with a perfectly wicked smile as he held himself propped up on his hands. I could almost feel his hard body against mine. Then, with his eyes never leaving mine, he lowered himself slowly, and I watched the head of my cock slide between his lips.

I moaned between my clenched teeth, hissing almost imperceptibly as I inhaled. Lying on my back, I opened the top drawer of my bedside table with one hand, blindly searching for the hand lotion, which I found easily by its distinctive shape. I brought it out, flipping the cap open as I closed the drawer with the back of my hand.

Holding myself steady with one hand, I squeezed the tube over the head and allowed a small measure of lotion to drizzle over my erection. Capping the container, I tossed it onto the bed and used both hands to spread the cool lotion over my hot skin. My right hand greased my shaft while the left concentrated on the head. It felt so fucking good. A soft whimper escaped me as my fingers danced over the ridges and grooves of my cock, just as I imagined his tongue might do. As my hips bucked up into my hand, I pictured his eager mouth around me.

Just then, another image came swiftly to mind. In another corner of the screen, I had seen one boy kneeling near the shoulders of another. I could almost see his hips jerking down, so that his cock was sliding in and out of the boy's mouth beneath him. I rolled over, getting up onto my knees and pitched forward onto my left forearm. My cheek rested against the cool fabric of my pillowcase as I reached down with my right hand to continue stroking. I spread my legs further so that my aching erection was almost touching the towel beneath me. Closing my eyes, I pictured Jamie's sweet face beneath me as I pumped into my hand.

Feeling so exposed in that position, I whimpered loudly between my clenched teeth, almost grunting in time with the motion of my hips. My legs spread, my ass in the air—almost as if I were waiting for him. It was then that I heard the slamming of a car door outside. I panicked for a second, knowing that there was no way I could stop. I stroked myself harder, paying particular attention to the head as I rocked my hips faster. My moans became unrestrained, and I turned my face into the pillow to contain them. Just as the front door closed, I cried out; the sound muffled by the pillow. I came in hard, jerking movements onto the towel beneath me, groaning long and low as the rest of my orgasm coursed through me.

The sound of footsteps on the stairs threw me into action. I leaned over and made sure I'd pushed my discarded clothes all the way under the bed. Grabbing the sheet and blanket, I jerked them up over me. I had just pressed my body against the semen-covered towel and my head had just hit the pillow when my door opened.

"Are you all right, Brian?" Carolyn asked as she stuck her head in my doorway. "The school called and said that you had run out of gym class before the last bell. No one knew what was wrong with you, and Coach Williams was worried." I looked over at her, feigning the most innocent expression that I could.

"I wasn't feeling well, so I came home to lie down," I mumbled, trying in vain to sound sick. It felt strange to be lying in my semen while talking to my foster mother. I really just wanted her to go downstairs so I could get cleaned up and dressed.

"You do look a little flushed; do you want me to bring you up anything?" she asked, guilt creeping through me at her motherly concern.

"No, I'm feeling better now. Maybe I was just overtired. I'll be down in a little while," I told her, laying my head back down on the pillow. She closed the door quietly, and I let out a sigh of relief. Remembering the feeling of a few minutes earlier, the best orgasm of my life, I moaned into the pillow.

CHAPTER THREE

The following Monday, I tried all day to speak with Jamie about what I had found during my Internet search. He'd been busy with yard work for most of the weekend, so we hadn't had a chance to get together, and this was certainly something I wasn't going to get into on the phone. I wanted him to know that maybe we weren't broken or wrong, maybe God didn't hate us. Maybe knowing that even scholars couldn't agree on whether or not being gay was a sin would help him sleep better at night. Unfortunately, whenever we had a few minutes to talk, we were always surrounded by people. I wasn't going to risk being overheard, not about this. Finally, during art, I was able to at least have a discussion with him about coming over after school.

During class, I still felt awkward around Mr. Barnes. *Now that Jamie and I had kissed, now that we had defined our relationship as something other than friendship, would he know? Did we give off a vibe like he did?* We were sitting side by side working on painting a bowl of plastic fruit. I tried not to notice the symbolism, but instead focused on the way Jamie's brush caressed the canvas, stroke after stroke. When I asked if I could come over, it made him happy. I liked that he didn't even care why I wanted to come over; he just seemed happy to be able to spend time with me.

We let our eyes lock for a little longer than was really necessary. When I caught myself and looked around, I realized with relief that no one had noticed. Criticizing myself immediately, it occurred to me that I was going to have to be more careful. After that, we worked on our projects in relative silence, only talking to ask for a different paint color or water. When class was over, we walked quickly to his house.

"Hi, Brian, you're looking better," Mrs. Mayfield greeted us as we came in through the back door. It took me a minute to figure out what she was talking about; church had been over a week ago, even though with all that Jamie and I had discovered, it seemed much longer. I must have looked fairly ill after the preacher's sermon for it to have made such an impression on her. Briefly, I wondered how many other of the preacher's flock had noticed me, pale and sick-looking, practically running from the "queers are going to hell" tirade.

"Yes, ma'am, I'm much better, thank you," I replied, smiling at her. Right now, I wanted nothing more than to be alone with Jamie. I was excited about what I had found and couldn't wait to share it with him. I wanted to talk to him and see if it answered as many questions for him as it did for me. However, Jamie was perfectly at ease and sat down at the kitchen table after grabbing a bag of chips from the cupboard. Giving him a meaningful look behind his mother's back, which wasn't difficult, as she was a rather large woman, Jamie looked back at me questioningly. Sighing, I pulled out a chair next to him and sat to have chips and a Coke with him. He was right, of course; we didn't want to seem too eager, and that was his afternoon ritual.

As his mama tied her hair back with a strip of some kind of cloth, she prattled on about a sweet elderly woman at church she wanted to take supper to. When she moved her hands, I saw that the strip of cloth must be denim because it matched her long denim skirt. It never ceased to amaze me how this woman always wore such long skirts, no matter how hot it was. Carolyn was perfectly comfortable in a T-shirt and cut-off shorts, but as far as I had seen, Mrs. Mayfield and a few of her church friends never even worn pants, much less shorts. Apparently, God wasn't a fan of jeans either. Thankfully, that didn't apply to Jamie. I wondered if Mr. Mayfield had interceded on his behalf.

Finally, Jamie put the chips away, and we went upstairs to start our homework. When we walked into his bedroom, I pulled his door almost closed and sat down on the bed near his desk. Jamie started to pull books out of his bag and laid them on the desk, but I put a hand on his arm.

"I have something for you," I told him quietly, but before I could open my bag to give him the printed papers, he caught my wrist in his hand. Glancing at the door, I looked back to give him a tentative smile.

"I bet you do," he said with a smirk, his voice low. The desire in his voice escalated the nervous excitement in my stomach, and I was too stunned to say anything. Then his lips were on mine. I moaned at the swiftness and urgency of his kiss. It was almost like he had been waiting all weekend to kiss me, to touch me. For all I knew, he had.

"Shhhhh... Mama's right downstairs," he said quietly as we broke apart. My body's response to his kiss took me by surprise. The attraction was definitely there, but to get so involved in the kiss with his mother right downstairs was dangerous. I didn't really know what had gotten into me. It seemed that with Jamie, I just lost track of my surroundings. *Were all relationships, all attractions, so intense?* Jamie didn't seem to lose his control with me. I didn't have time to really ponder what that meant.

"Sorry," I whispered and then cleared my throat as I pulled the papers out of my bag. "I really do have something for you." He looked sheepish for a moment, and it was my turn to smirk. Taking the papers from me, he sat down on his bed and started to read. I did not interrupt him as he took his time getting through all the pages. I just sat quietly and watched his changing facial expressions. Mostly, he looked puzzled, but a few times, he smirked at the content and even outright smiled. I couldn't help but smile with him. When he was finished, he handed them back to me.

"Well, that helps. I mean, if the pastors and priests and such can't agree, then it's really a matter of interpretation," he remarked quietly. "Did you find anything else?" I knew that he meant something like the reference materials I'd given him, but I couldn't help but remember all of the images from the site I'd found, and I blushed scarlet. He looked at me wide-eyed. "What else did you find?" I looked at the floor, and he pulled me to stand just behind the bedroom door so that if anyone opened it wider, it would hit him and stop them from walking in on us.

Pressing his body against mine, he whispered in my ear, "Did you find something naughty, Brian?"

I swallowed once and nodded. My heart was pounding, and I was more than a little embarrassed talking to him about this. I mean, I'd kind of admitted to looking at porn on the Internet. Only creepy guys in their basements did that, right? Before I could feel too weird about it, he asked, "Will you tell me about what you found?"

In a hushed voice, I told him about the images I had seen on the screen, not mentioning the fact that the blond boy reminded me so much of him that I'd masturbated to the image. I felt ashamed talking about it in the first place without telling him that I wanted him to do those things to me. Being purposely vague, I described the boys and their positions. As I spoke, I felt his breathing start to accelerate on my cheek. With his body against mine, I felt him getting hard as his erection pressed against my stomach, which tightened in excitement. He was several inches taller than I was, and standing like that, he was pressed right against my navel.

"Jamie!" Mrs. Mayfield called up the stairs, and we jumped apart as if on fire. Our faces flamed slightly in embarrassment and guilt when we looked at each other. Then, he moved so that I could come out from behind the door. As he opened it, he called downstairs.

"Yes, Mama?" His voice was a little higher-pitched than usual, excited. I took several deep breaths, willing my erection to go away.

"Will Brian be staying for dinner?" He looked at me, and I shook my head vigorously, as I didn't think I'd be able to stand being at the dinner table with Jamie and his parents after what had just happened. I knew I wouldn't be able to keep my face impassive; I'd blush and stammer, and they'd know that something was up. I was probably being paranoid, but I was still hard and wasn't thinking clearly.

"No, he's gonna head home," he yelled back and then pulled the door closed again after hearing her acknowledgement. He looked at me for a long time. "Are you going to run again?"

I shook my head slowly. Sure, I was nervous. Our relationship was moving to a whole different level. But I couldn't pretend to be saddened by it. He took my hand and led me over to his bed. As soon as we were seated, he let go of my hand, and the disappointment flared within me. We sat there, side by side, neither of us apparently willing to break the silence. He was looking at his hands in his lap. I turned slightly, pulling my knee up between us so that I was facing him, and then he did the same.

"Jamie, you and I have been friends since we were eleven. For a while now, I've been feeling something else for you. I like you, as more than just a friend, and that scares the hell out of me. It scares me because if I like you that way, it means that I'm gay, and I don't want to be gay. It scares me because if this doesn't work out, I could lose you, and I don't want that to happen. I have to guess that you feel the same way about me, since you kissed me on Friday?" I paused, and he nodded, and I felt a wave of happiness wash through me at his admission. He still looked nervous, almost anxious, like what I'd said hadn't truly registered. "We will have to hide this from everybody. If anyone finds out, it could be really bad for us." Then, to my surprise, rather than being more upset at the thought of things going badly for us, he looked relieved, and maybe even a little shy. It really looked like he wanted whatever it was that was happening between us to work, and for the first time since I'd started to suspect that I was gay, I felt some measure of hope.

Putting his hand on my face, he traced the contours of my cheek, his eyes holding mine, and after a while he spoke. "It is worth it. I've never met anyone who makes me feel the way that you do. I would rather have this"—he gestured quickly between us—"as a secret than not have it at all." I nodded, telling him that I wanted it too. Then, at the same time, we both leaned forward slowly, and I closed my eyes, feeling the tender touch of his kiss. It was sealing our promise to each other, the promise that we would try.

I had thought that the rest of the week would be nearly impossible to endure, but it wasn't. The knowledge that I wasn't alone, that Jamie was right there beside me, made things much easier. The week that I had spent trying to hide from the one person who knew me better than I knew myself had been exhausting. Jamie and I did, however, spend the week being extraordinarily careful about our interactions, sometimes ridiculously so. When I reached over during woodshop on Tuesday for the sandpaper and our hands touched, I jerked back like his skin was made of hot coal. He looked at me curiously, but then went on with his project.

I found myself distracted by the way his hands moved over the wood. The pads of his fingertips glided gracefully over the grainy surface, seeking out imperfections and finding none. I had a fleeting image of his fingers inspecting the contours of my body just as thoroughly, and then forced my mind to focus on something else. It wouldn't have been good to sport wood, even if it was woodshop.

For the next several days, we continued to avoid physical contact and worked to keep our conversations and expressions neutral. To be honest, it was an arduous exercise, to think about every step, every movement all day long and wonder how others would interpret it. By Friday, I was ecstatic to be out of school and away from the prying eyes that seemed to follow Jamie and me everywhere we went. I sounded paranoid because I was paranoid; our whole lives could change in an instant if anyone found out. I didn't know how I was going to live like that every day until the school year ended. Once that last day was behind us, we could hide over the summer, in each other's arms, until classes started in the fall. We were both juniors; we had one more year until we would be free.

I came in through the back door on Friday afternoon, and Carolyn smiled at me. I smiled back, still feeling guilty about the previous Friday. The lies I had told her about why I had left gym had caused me to not only clean the gutters for Richard but scrub the oven for Carolyn. My sweet foster mother had given me an odd look as I knelt in front of the ancient stove with the oven cleaner and a rag, but she'd long since gotten used to my eccentricities. When I was first placed with them, I used to clean at random during all hours of the day and night. The therapist that the state had hired to evaluate me before I came to the Schreibers' said that it was an involuntary reaction to stress. All I knew was that it took my mind off of things and made my foster parents happy, which was what mattered to me.

That weekend was going to be both heaven and hell for me. Jamie and his parents had gone on a church retreat, so I wasn't going to see him until school on Monday. I hoped that would give me enough time without his ever-pervasive presence to work out what was going on in my head. I was going to try to work out a plan on how to react around him in front of other people without losing my train of thought. Not only did I need to work things out in my own head, but I also wanted to talk to him about both my fears and my feelings. The problem, the hell part of the equation, lay in his absence. I was going to miss him terribly.

Honestly, I wasn't going to miss him only because I wanted to talk to him. I was going to miss his soft breath just behind my ear as he tried to gain control of himself after a meaningful kiss. I was going to miss his quirky grins at the most insignificant things and the way he tapped his fingers in a senseless rhythm on his knee while waiting for me to respond to a question. There were thousands of little things about Jamie that contributed to the incredibly amazing person that he was. I was going to miss each and every one.

Friday night I passed the time by doing every single piece of homework I'd been assigned, finally falling exhausted into bed around two in the morning. I stayed in bed for a long time on Saturday morning, holding on to the dream of him, the essence of him, for as long as I could. By Saturday night, I was anxious. Even the tremendous amount of yard work that I'd volunteered to help Richard with could not exhaust me enough to make me relax. My body was tired, but my mind raced. With everything that had happened in the last week, I felt anxious without him.

Unable to concentrate on anything specific, I lay on my bed. Jamie's face swam before my eyes, and I just wanted to touch him and hear his voice. Any doubt about my feelings for Jamie had disappeared that day as I struggled to keep myself from going to his house and sitting in the tree house just to feel close to him. My biggest fear was that he would come to the realization that the risk of us together wasn't worth it. He was surrounded by people who hated and feared people like us. *What if they convinced him that what we were doing was wrong? What if he came back and didn't want to be with me anymore? Or worse, what if he came back and hated me just like the rest of them?*

By Sunday afternoon I had started to make Carolyn edgy. She gave me ten dollars and told me to go to the arcade down on Fifth Street. When the phone rang on Sunday evening, Carolyn gave me a strange look as I nearly vaulted over a low table in order to pick up the receiver—so much for subtlety. I couldn't stand not knowing what was going through his head. It seemed what little confidence I had gained in the last few weeks had dissipated in his absence.

"Hello?" I asked breathlessly before the phone was even all the way up to my ear. Deep down, I had known that it would be Jamie. I briefly wondered if he felt the same uneasiness I did when we weren't together.

"Hey, Bri, we just got in," he said jovially, like there was no one else he would rather talk to in that moment than me. My chest filled with a warmth that I had never felt, and the anxious knot in my stomach started to loosen. I imagined him reclining on one of his kitchen chairs, his face lit up with one of his brilliant smiles.

"How was your outing?" I asked with mild interest. If he was calling me as soon as he got home, sounding like he'd really missed me, then obviously they hadn't changed his mind about wanting to be with me, as I had feared almost constantly throughout the last forty-eight hours.

"It was okay."

I could almost hear the shrug I was sure came with that statement. Knowing Jamie as I did, that meant they had talked about some tough subjects for him, but he was just playing it casual.

"I was wondering if you could come by before school tomorrow," he whispered.

"Sure, is everything okay?" I asked, my heart suddenly in my throat. *Maybe he wasn't playing casual, maybe he wanted out.*

"I missed you; I just want to see you," he explained, still whispering. Pure, unadulterated joy filled me at his admission. "I'll meet you in the tree house."

"I'd love to spend some time alone with you before school tomorrow," I told him honestly. Before hanging up, we talked for a few more minutes, at normal volume, about mundane things like homework and a new song he'd heard on the radio. I almost floated up the stairs when it was time to go to bed. In just a few more hours, I was finally going to be in his arms again.

The next morning, I rushed through my routine and, before running full speed out of the back door, called to Carolyn that I had a project due that I needed to finish. I wasn't sure she'd bought it, but right then, it didn't matter. When I got to the Mayfields', I opened the back gate quietly and sprinted for the tree house ladder, feeling like some kind of spy. Not wanting Jamie's parents to catch me, to have to explain why I was in their tree house, I bolted up the ladder and was unsurprised to find it empty. Jamie always took more time to get ready for school than I did.

Glancing around the small space, I noticed a worn quilt lying in the corner that I didn't remember having been there during our rainy day revelations. Just as I was about to go investigate, I heard Jamie climbing the ladder to the tree house. Moving back from the entrance, I saw his head pop up through the trapdoor, and I smiled. He smiled back and pulled himself up, careful not to rip his good jeans on one of the exposed nails jutting from the floorboards. Even though that was the style, his mother would have been furious if he had ripped perfectly good jeans.

"Hi," he said, almost shyly, like he was as scared as I was about our secret meeting. There was no reason to be scared, of course. Jamie and I were generally described as inseparable, but the guilt that I felt, like we weren't supposed to be doing this, weighed on me. The purpose of the meeting, affection and attraction, and possibly its location were what made it scandalous.

"Hi," was my witty response as he straightened up in the small space, his face now inches from mine. We stood awkwardly, just looking at each other. Every few seconds, I would shift my weight slightly from one foot to the other, waiting for something to happen. Finally, when I realized that nothing was going to happen, I asked him about the blanket to distract us from the almost uneasy silence that was permeating the tree house.

"Oh," he said, and moved past me to pick it up. "I brought it out here last night so that we could spread it on the floor when we're up here and not get dirty." Something in me lifted at the thought of spending hours in this place, alone and free, with him. It didn't matter if we were talking, or kissing, or even playing a board game as long as we were spending time together. He opened up the blanket and spread it out, taking up nearly half of the floor space. In the back of my mind, I started to make a list of other things we could bring up here.

"That was a great idea, Jamie." We had about twenty minutes before we had to leave for school, so I took off my ratty gym shoes that at one time had been white, and sat on the blanket facing him as he sat, not bothering with his shoes. We were both sitting with our legs crossed in front of us. When he looked at me, I noticed he had a piece of white fuzz from the blanket in his hair. Reaching forward, I pulled it out, and he caught my hand, holding it gently.

"Is it wrong to tell you that I missed you this weekend?" he asked quietly, first looking down at the blanket, then up at me. I shook my head and, using his grip on my hand, pulled him closer to me. My heart leapt with his admission and with his nearness. I could feel his breath on my face, and I wanted nothing more than to stay in this moment, this perfect moment of anticipation.

"No, I... well, I like that you missed me," I admitted, and then with my lips almost at the pulse point below his ear, continued, "because I wanted so badly to see you." Turning his head slightly, his lips sought mine hungrily. As I felt them find their mark, I wound my fingers into his silky hair, accidentally pulling it when I shifted my weight slightly, causing him to moan desperately into my mouth.

I hadn't realized he was pushing me back onto the blanket until he was on top of me. All rational thought left me in that moment. Picturing the images I had seen on Richard's computer screen, I pressed my hips up into his, my blossoming erection pushing against the crotch of his jeans, and I whimpered slightly as his lips moved to my neck.

"Jamie," I groaned breathlessly as I felt his hips move lightly against mine. Barely pulling up my T-shirt, one of his hands leisurely rubbed the small of my back while the other remained on my neck. With both hands in his hair, I wrapped one of my legs up over his, pulling him harder against me. It felt so fucking good to be in his arms, to feel his need for me. The need that was almost as strong as my need for him. My heart was racing as I reached down and pulled his shirt up. Immediately, he pulled back just enough to break the kiss.

"Brian, we can't. As much as I want to keep going, we have to go to school," he panted into my neck, his body still pressed hard against mine. I nodded, on the verge of asking him if we could just skip. Unfortunately, with everything else we were trying to work out, being caught playing hooky would not be a good idea. Thinking about what we had to talk about brought to mind a question I had been meaning to ask.

"Jamie, what are we?" My voice trembled a little in my nervousness. I didn't know why the answer to that question was so important to me, but it was. I had to know that he was in it for the long haul, that our relationship wasn't just some kind of phase or experiment. Pulling back to look at me, his eyes searched mine.

"Brian, you were my best friend. Now, you are so much more to me. I know that we aren't ready to be too serious yet, that everything is just so new, but I want this to work between us. Once we're ready, then we would be, what, boyfriends?" He smiled as he said it, and I felt like I was dancing inside. It was everything that I could have wanted. I pulled him down to me and kissed him again. It was a slow, sweet kiss full of my love, acceptance, and promise.

"We should get to school," I told him with a sigh. It was one of the last things I wanted to do, but it was a necessity. He gave me one final small kiss, just barely pressing his lips against mine before standing up and holding his hand out to me. Hoisting me up next to him, he held on to my hand a little longer than necessary before scooping up my shoes and handing them to me.

"Will you stay over Saturday night?" he asked hopefully, like I would ever want to be anywhere else.

As we always did, Jamie and I sat next toeach other at the lunch table with about half a dozen assorted friends. Derrick Kennedy and John Kurtz were across from us talking about some video game they were going to get after school. Kurtz's girlfriend Tara was steadfastly ignoring him in some kind of girlish pout because she wasn't invited on their boys' night out. She was flipping through some flashy teen magazine with the latest heartthrob of the week splashed across the front. She sat next to me in math, and the guy on the cover distracted me all through class with his full pouty lips and big green eyes. I had only stopped looking at the cover when Jamie had caught my eye and smirked.

"Hey Mayfield, you want to head over to Northridge Mall with us after school for a while?" Kennedy asked Jamie. After glancing up at them once, I pretended to study my mystery meat sandwich. Kennedy wasn't talking to me. It was generally understood by me and by them that I was just Jamie's little tagalong geek friend. I wasn't one of the popular kids; I was just the throwaway foster kid, though that had never mattered to Jamie. In fact, he'd told me that was one of the things that made me special, the fact that I never took anything for granted.

"Can Brian come?" Jamie asked casually. They knew as well as I did that his answer would depend on theirs. If they said no, so would he. Kennedy looked at me for a minute, and I saw the effort it took him not to sigh before he agreed.

"Sure, we'll meet you out front after last bell. My mom let me take the car, so we can go straight from here," he said. Jamie and I threw our garbage in the bin and tossed our trays up on the belt for the lunch ladies to get.

"Do you want to go to the mall after school?" Jamie asked me as we headed to our lockers to get our books for our next class.

"You already told them we'd go, why are you asking me now?" I asked, a little frustrated at being an afterthought. I reached my locker with him lagging several steps behind and tossed the books for our next two classes into my bag along with folders and notebooks. Just for good measure, so that I wouldn't have to look up at him, I made sure I had pens and pencils as well.

"Because if you want to do something else, I'll tell them to fuck off," he replied, lowering his voice as a couple of girls passed. "Come on, a couple more weeks until we're done this year, and then we'll be seniors, and then we'll be gone. Once we're in college, we can start over and be who we want to be. It will be a new beginning for us. We just have to get the fuck out of here first." I was a little stunned at his tone. Jamie never swore like that. So, rather than argue, I just agreed to meet him in front of the school after the last bell.

The rest of the school day passed surprisingly quickly. We were gearing up for final exams and final projects, so the teachers were pretty relentless during classes. More work and constant talk of making sure we pass to get to senior year made our minds focus more and wander less. By the end of the day, the mall seemed like a pretty good diversion.

"Ready to go?" he asked with that soft, sweet smile, the one that made my heart race.

"Yeah, are we just leaving our books in Derrick's car?" I asked. Not really having any friends other than Jamie, sometimes I felt left out: *like a shadow standing next to him, a flat, two-dimensional representation of a boy not really good enough to—*

"Hey, whatever you're thinking, just stop," Jamie said sternly, and I looked up from my shoes. "We don't have to stay with those guys the whole time. I just want to hang out with you. Okay?"

Wishing that we could have just been alone, I nodded and glanced up the hall to see a couple of younger girls walking past. Jamie was one of the popular kids, and he didn't understand what it was like to be forced on people who didn't want you around. My entire life had been like that, until Jamie. Jamie wanted me, but he'd also been friends with guys like John and Derrick since kindergarten. I couldn't just isolate him from his other friends because they didn't think I was good enough for him. Besides, it was the chance to spend time with Jamie someplace that wasn't at school or with our parents. That was enough for me to put one foot in front of the other and follow him to his friend's car.

The half-hour ride up to Northridge Mall was pretty uneventful. Derrick and John were in the front seat, talking about which girls at our high school put out and about girls they might see from North Central, a high school near the mall. For the most part Jamie and I ignored them, not joining in their conversation with more than a "yeah" or a "no way" when appropriate. I was starting to wonder why I had agreed to this straight boy bonding trip when we finally pulled off of the highway and turned toward the mall.

The first half an hour was spent wandering around the video game shop, but since I had neither a game console nor a computer, I wasn't really interested. When we moved on to a music store, I followed Jamie from display to display, watching him get increasingly bored because I knew for a fact that he bought most of his music online. We wandered over and looked through a few band T-shirts. As I held up a particularly lurid green one under the pretense of asking Jamie's opinion, I leaned in closer to him.

"Let's go to the bookstore," I said quietly, and he nodded, grabbing the T-shirt and putting it back on the rack. Derrick and John, while great on the football field, had probably never been inside of a bookstore. They'd much rather hang out with Brad Mosely and Ryan Carter chugging beers while sitting in the back of Mosely's pickup truck or beating each other's brains in on the fifty yard line than actually read.

"Hey, D!" Jamie called, and Derrick turned away from the pretty store employee, looking annoyed by the interruption.

"We're gonna head over to the bookstore. Meet you in the food court in an hour?" Jamie asked, and Derrick waved him off with a nod.

We were free.

Nearly sprinting to the front of the store, we escaped the blaring music and turned right, heading in the direction of the large bookstore near the elevators. Once out of the deafening music, we walked slower. It was nice to simply be together, taking in the storefronts and other shoppers. Since it was a Thursday afternoon, the mall was pretty empty.

Jamie leaned down as we passed the pink-frilled door of a lingerie shop and whispered, "Maybe we should go in there and see if we can find you something sexy, silk, maybe? They have stuff for guys too." My face flamed at the thought of wearing sexy underwear for him, and then again at Carolyn finding them, and I shook my head. He laughed, and when I realized that he was just teasing me, I laughed along with him.

"Only if I get to blow you in the changing room," I countered, and he immediately stopped laughing and walking, just staring at me. To my credit, I kept a straight face as he gawked at me. I could tell that he'd never, ever thought he'd hear his shy little friend even joke about something like that, especially as hard as I had blushed when I had told him about the porn I'd found on the computer.

"I thought you wanted to go to the bookstore?" I asked him casually when he didn't show any signs of remembering why we were walking at the mall. His feet started moving again, and I hid a smirk as I waited for him to catch up, and walked next to him. He didn't say anything until we were a few stores down, hip hop blaring from the sports clothing store as we passed.

"Would you really?" he asked quietly.

"Do you mean in general, or in a dressing room?" I clarified quickly.

"In general," he hedged as we passed a large jewelry store.

"It's something I would like to try with you," I told him honestly. "It's something I've thought about." I looked around to make sure that no one was within earshot. "It's something I've fantasized about... a lot." I hadn't meant to say that last part, but it was true.

"I have, too," he whispered as we walked into the huge two-story bookstore at the end of the corridor. Out of habit, I went over to the clearance section and started checking out the paperbacks. I looked over my shoulder and saw that Jamie had gone farther down the aisle into science fiction. Picking through the haphazardly stacked piles of books, I found one by an author that I liked and went to find two chairs next to each other so that when Jamie found something we could sit together.

I dropped into the worn leather chair and started to read the back of the novel. It promised to be every bit as good as the last book I'd read by the author, full of intrigue and the triumph over adversity. I knew that not everyone triumphed, but it was nice to read about, even if it was just fiction. The music being piped through the in-store speakers was soothing, and when Jamie finally joined me, I'd already finished the first chapter.

He had a bag with him, which meant he'd already paid for his books. When I asked him about them, he just shrugged, dropped into his chair, and took one out of the bag. It was the new hardback novel by John Marshall, the same author I was reading.

"I didn't know you were a fan of Marshall's work," Jamie said as he noticed the book in my hands. "It's funny, there are books all over your room, and I've never taken the time to find out what they were."

"I didn't know you were a fan either. You... well, you don't have any books in your room," I said, a little sheepishly because I had always assumed that just meant that Jamie wasn't a reader.

"That's because I keep my books in my dad's study. He has tons of bookshelves in there."

"What else did you get?" I asked, curious to see if we had any other common interests that we didn't know about. I thought after being best friends for almost six years that we knew everything about each other. Apparently, I was wrong. However, Jamie didn't let go of the bag and wouldn't let me look in it.

"It's nothing," he insisted, and the note of urgency in his voice made me stop. Obviously there was something in that bag that he was either embarrassed about or that he didn't want me to see. Immediately, I let go of the bag, and he relaxed a little back into the chair, pushing his soft hair back from his eyes. A ton of possibilities, from gay-related books to sex-related books, chased each other through my mind as I tried to figure out what he was hiding.

Nervously, he checked his watch. "Hey, we've got to go; we're supposed to be in the food court to meet Derrick and John," he said as he pulled himself out of the chair. I tossed the paperback in my chair as I stood, and together we made our way to the door.

"Aren't you going to get that paperback you started reading?" Jamie asked curiously as we left the store.

"Don't you have it?" I asked casually.

"Yeah, I have it." He turned the corner and headed back in the direction we'd come.

"Then I'll just borrow yours," I told him with a smirk. He grinned sheepishly as we passed the jewelry store again.

"You're such a cheapskate." He said, chuckling to himself, and pulled his bag from the bookstore up, hoisting it over his shoulder.

"Being a cheapskate will help me pay for college," I told him. There was nothing from my parents. Either they hadn't had anything, or it'd gone to the state for my care. If I wanted to go to college, I would have to find the money. Being the only child of a middle class family, I didn't think Jamie really understood that. He also never understood why I wouldn't just let him buy the book, or the CD, or even the bag of chips, for me. When it came to matters of money, Jamie and I generally stood at an impasse.

"Of course you can borrow the book," he said quietly as we walked quickly past the lingerie shop, and I remembered our earlier discussion with a grin. I could tell that Jamie had remembered too because he was blushing.

The food court was relatively empty, so we didn't have any trouble finding the guys, who were feasting on Chinese. Jamie and I waved to get their attention and motioned that we were going to get food as well.

It had been a nice, quiet time, nothing special in the grand scheme of a teenager's social calendar, but I liked being able to spend time with Jamie that was someplace other than school. The constant twittering of girls, the slamming of lockers, and the mocking laughter that followed me whenever I wasn't with Jamie was absent from the low bustle of the mall.

It made me long for the school year to end.

CHAPTER FOUR

"Jamie, I don't think we should be doing this with your parents right down the hall," I told him between fevered kisses as we lay on the inflatable mattress that his parents always put out for me. It was comfortable and just a few feet away from Jamie's own twin captain's bed, which had a lot of his character. From the handsome yet functional bookcase headboard to the calming blue plaid comforter freshly laid across its surface. One of the things I loved most about his bed was lying on it while we did our homework together, and his scent would envelop me, and I could torture myself with the image of him lying naked in bed with me.

"You know as well as I do that they won't come to check on us this late. They're asleep, and if they're not, they think we are." He cocked his head to the side, and his face fell a bit. "Unless you don't want to?"

I responded by using my arms that were still around his neck to pull his face back to mine. We were facing each other as we lay on our sides, wearing just our twisted and tented pajama pants. Our long-discarded shirts lay rumpled and forgotten, entwined under his desk. Excited and a little apprehensive, I rushed headlong into my first real sexual experience without any thought for what would happen after. All I wanted to think about was the feeling of his mouth melded with mine, or his hands as he rubbed my bare skin.

It was beautiful and sensual.

I wrapped my leg around his and pulled it between both of my mine, feeling my eager erection press against his thigh as his pressed into my hip. The friction, coupled with the emotion that flowed between us, made it the best sexual experience I'd ever had. It was already incredible, and I hadn't even gotten off yet. Slowly but deliberately, he began to grind his hips against mine, intensifying my need for him, and he emitted soft, mewling whimpers. His excitement just escalated my own. I nearly lost all control of myself when, after sliding his hand down and grabbing my ass for leverage, he gasped, "Oh God, Brian," almost too quietly for me to hear. Those desperate sounds of pleasure, of sheer need, nearly made me come in my baseball-themed pajama pants.

I had no idea where it was leading; all I knew for sure was that I never wanted it to stop.

A noise in the hall drew our attention. After a brief look at me, during which I nodded my head frantically to indicate I had heard it as well, Jamie scrambled out of my arms, stood, and dove onto his bed. We both jerked the blankets over ourselves, feigning sleep. No one entered Jamie's room, but it was several minutes before I heard anything else, and what I heard brought my erection back in full force.

The sound was Jamie's labored breathing.

"Jamie," I whispered, "are you...." I trailed off. I just couldn't force myself to say "masturbating," or even "jacking off." It didn't matter though. He knew what I meant.

"Uh huh," he replied in a low moan. Again, that excitement, that need, pulsed through me, making my already hard cock throb. Silently, I lifted myself up and pulled my sleep pants down so that the waistband was around my upper thighs and I was exposed. I stroked myself lightly as I listened to him. Then I rolled onto my side and watched his profile in the moonlight that came in from the nearby window. I could see movement under his blanket, but I also saw his other hand rubbing his chest. *Did that make it better?*

Tentatively, I brought my right hand up to my chest while my left was still wrapped tightly around my hard-on. My hips jerked as I rolled one nipple between my thumb and forefinger. It was almost as if there were a single electric current from my nipple straight down through my stomach. The small slapping sounds coming from the other bed were making me crazy while I watched him. Jamie's head was pressed back into his pillow, and from what I could see in the dim light, his eyes were closed. Having progressed from labored breathing to harsh, ragged pants, it was obvious that he was close to reaching his peak. The blanket rose and fell rapidly, and his blond hair was matted on his forehead, either from exertion or the extraordinarily warm spring night. My heart nearly stopped when, without slowing his piston-like hand, he used the other to push down his blankets. I wasn't sure if he did it because he knew I was watching or to keep them from being soiled.

With a deep, poorly contained groan, his back arched and his hand slowed to uncontrolled movements. Sharp, hoarse gasps accompanied the jerky rhythm of his strokes, and I imagined his semen landing across his flat stomach. His hand, which had been a blur the moment before, slowed to a languid rhythm as his orgasm began to wane.

It was the most erotic thing I had ever witnessed. In the silence that followed, I felt so much closer to him for sharing that deeply intimate act with me. The wild impulse to crawl into bed and curl around him was almost overpowering, but I held back. We could never take that kind of chance.

Then he turned to look at me, and our eyes met. The playfulness and hunger in his expression told me that it was my turn to share. I felt immediately self-conscious about my lewd display. For some reason, watching Jamie was beautiful, but I felt a little guilty about letting him watch me. It suddenly felt like we were doing something wrong. However, I knew that he would love watching me as I had him. So I put my fear, shame, and pajama pants aside, and I masturbated for Jamie. His look of hunger and something else I couldn't quite understand were worth the slight embarrassment of jacking off in front of someone else. I had to admit, however, that the thought of him watching me really fucking turned me on. *Did my sounds, my inability to control my own desire, make him excited?*

As my cock throbbed, all I could think about was straddling his perfect face, seeing it between my legs as I looked down at him. I wanted to feel his lips, his tongue on my balls while I stroked. Damn, I was so close, and I knew he could tell as I tried to keep my whimpers quiet. If he ever did actually suck me off, if we ever got that chance, as much as I imagined the scene, it would take only seconds for me to come. Kind of like masturbating in front of him, God, I was close.

Afterwards, we both cleaned up with our discarded T-shirts, and after a fairly awkward goodnight, we fell asleep.

We didn't talk the next morning about our shared experience, but I think both of us realized that we had crossed a certain line in our relationship. No longer just friends, we were officially something more, something yet to be defined.

It wasn't until Jamie's mother came to wake us that I remembered about church. As she closed the door, reminding us that we only had fifteen more minutes before we had to get up, I rolled over to face the opposite wall, faintly sick. Jamie guessedwhat was bothering me. He slid out of bed and quickly climbed onto the mattress beside me. I felt his hand slide over my bare stomach, and I shivered.

"Jamie, you can't be here; what if your mother comes back?" I didn't have the strength to roll and face him, so I pulled my knees up to my chest and continued to stare at the wall. We were going to have to sit there, side by side, listening to how much God hated us and how even though Jamie was such a good person, he was going to hell right along with me. I didn't know if I could stand sitting through that again.

"Brian," he said while his hand came up to stroke my hair. "He just did a sermon on that; he's not going to do another one again so soon. Besides, we know it isn't true. Don't listen to what he says. We know in our hearts we're supposed to be together." At that, I rolled over to face him, and his lips quickly descended to mine before he got off my makeshift bed. I lay there for a few more minutes, thinking about what he'd said as he went to shower. Jamie was right, of course. Nothing that the preacher had said, or was going to say, would have made any difference to us.

Rather than worry about what would or wouldn't happen that morning, I decided to imagine being in the shower with Jamie.

As it turned out, the pastor's sermon wasn't about homosexuality. Instead he preached about adultery. Apparently, someone's secretary had been caught in bed with someone else's husband. The scandal was all over the church. Men talked about it in low voices behind their copies of the hymnal while women gossiped more openly in the doorway. It was a feeding frenzy, and the sharks were in prime form. With a mounting sense of unease, I wondered what kind of frenzy they would go into over Jamie and me. *Which was the worse sin: being a whore, an adulterer, or a fag?*

After the service, while we were getting ready to leave, two of our friends from school, Karen Simmons and Emma Mosely, came by to say hi. Emma, the smaller, shy, soft-spoken girl with glasses and frizzy brown hair, kept sneaking furtive glances at Jamie. She had an annoying habit of dissolving into a fit of giggles each time his gaze fell upon her. Karen, on the other hand, was a bigger girl with a loud, grating voice. Her black hair fell in waves around her boyish face, and she moved awkwardly in the heeled shoes she apparently wore only on Sunday. Today, her acne was acting up again, and it was hard to draw my eyes away from the torrent of purplish spots along her cheeks and chin.

Mrs. Mayfield beamed as she watched the exchange between Jamie and Emma, and I got the feeling that she had sent the girls over to us. It was obvious that Emma was attracted to Jamie. I mean hell, who wouldn't be? He was smart, sweet, and beautiful. Mrs. Mayfield was obviously pleased that such a wholesome, churchgoing girl was interested in her boy. Then they could get married, live in town, and have a dozen wholesome, churchgoing babies.

"Hi, Brian," Karen said, sidling up next to me, her voice a little loud to be polite for post-church chatter. I wasn't sure if she was interested in me as much as she was interested in getting Emma and Jamie together. They had never displayed this kind of attention in the cafeteria at lunch. Maybe they had just worked up the courage, or maybe there were fewer teenage witnesses at church. More likely, however, was the idea that Jamie's mother had given them a little pep talk. In any event, they were working their advantage.

"Hi, Karen," I mumbled, wondering how I could put off a vibe that said "not interested" without actually giving myself away.

While making small talk with this overly enthusiastic girl about her quest to become first chair in band, I happened to look over and notice that Jamie was flirting with Emma. He was smiling that secretive campy smile that I thought he saved for me, and then he pushed her frizzy hair back behind her ear. Something in me broke as I watched the exchange. I excused myself quickly, thanking Mrs. Mayfield for letting me stay as I walked purposefully toward the door. Jamie tried calling me back, but I never slowed.

He called my house three times that day, and each time I asked Carolyn to tell him that I was unavailable. Technically, that was true, because I had a lot to think about. *What if Jamie wasn't gay? What if it was just some different form of our deeper friendship and I was keeping him from a much less complicated life?* He could go on to marry a girl, have kids, and be normal. With me, the only thing he could look forward to was a life of hardship and ridicule. On the other hand,

I thought after last night things had changed between us. I thought that we were becoming closer, that we were becoming more than just friends. For him to flirt with someone else right in front of me was like a slap in the face, and I didn't appreciate it. I hated feeling so damn insecure all the time, so unsure about Jamie. It would be funny if it weren't so fucking dangerous.

When he called the final time, he left a message, and Carolyn came up to my room to deliver it.

"Brian, darlin', Jamie called again. I don't know what kind of disagreement you boys had, but he wants you to meet him tomorrow before school so y'all can talk." She came over and sat on the bed next to me before continuing. "You and I know that I'm not your real mama, but I love you just the same." I looked up at her, startled. It was the first time she had ever said those words to me. "I know that I'm not supposed to get attached to the children who stay with us. Richard says that only leads to a broken heart for me, but with you, I can't help it."

Deep down, I really wanted to tell her about Jamie and me, to finally be able to let it out. I just couldn't stand to see the disappointment in her face, especially right after her admission.

"You're the only person I can remember ever wanting to call Mama, Carolyn. I don't remember my own mother at all, and you've treated me better, with more care and respect than I've ever had," I told her sincerely, because I meant every single word. "I wish I could talk about what's been wrong lately, but I just can't bring myself to do it."

"I can understand that. We all have our demons, Brian. When you're ready, I'll be here." I nodded, and she gave me a quick hug before leaving the room and heading back downstairs.

Shuffling through my room aimlessly, I got my school bag ready for the next day, changed into my pajamas, and lay down on my bed. The cracks in the ceiling were almost mocking me as I tried in vain to sleep.

The night felt like it had lasted an entire week, but eventually Monday morning dawned with muggy slowness. As I watched, the sun rose outside my bedroom window, creeping higher and higher, obliterating the darkness where I could hide my insecurities. Finally, I rolled out of bed to escape its bright and cheery implications of the new day. I knew he wanted me to meet him at the tree house, so I planned on getting there about an hour before we had to leave for school.

When I was dressed, I grabbed my backpack and headed downstairs. Reaching the first floor, I saw Carolyn sitting at the table, waiting to make me breakfast. I was surprised; I thought for sure she would still be asleep.

"You're up early," I commented as I shuffled into the kitchen and tossed my bag onto one of the empty chairs.

"Jamie wanted to talk to you before school. I figured you'd be up early." Too tired and full of trepidation to make small talk, I stared morosely at the smooth, polished tabletop. In no time at all, it seemed, a plate of bacon and scrambled eggs appeared in the spot at which I had been staring. As she passed to go back upstairs to wake Richard, she ruffled my long, barely controlled hair.

"Whatever it is that's going on with you and Jamie, just remember that some misunderstandings look entirely different in the light of a new day."

I nodded, knowing that she was right. Looking back at the situation yesterday with Jamie and Emma, I had probably overreacted and let my jealousy get the better of me. It was just so unsettling not to be sure of his feelings for me, or his intentions. While he had said that he wanted us to be together, if the stress got to be too much, he could easily change his mind about me. He could just decide that the foster kid charity case just wasn't worth the hassle.

That thought was like a stabbing pain in my chest.

Scraping and rinsing my breakfast dishes quickly, I headed out the back door and took a left into the alley at the end of the sidewalk. My feet instinctively knew to take me to Jamie's house; it was the place I went more often than any other.

Occasionally, I saw men heading for their cars, going off to work, and I saw Karen Simmons's kid brother delivering the morning paper on his old dirt bike. Mostly though, it was very quiet on the short walk to the Mayfields' house. The silence was broken only by the sound of early morning sprinklers in their perfectly synchronized watering of well-cared for lawns.

By the time I had reached the end of our alley and turned onto Elm Street for the four-block walk to Jamie's house, I had decided that the very first thing I would do when he finally got into the tree house was apologize. Jamie was always late—to school, to church, probably even to his own funeral when the time came.

My spirits had been lifted, the weight off of my shoulders by the time I reached his back gate. I was being stupid, and I was going tell him that. Lifting the latch up quietly, I swung the chain link gate open. Being careful to close it behind me, I walked over to the tree house ladder. Luckily, there were no signs of life from the house. No one needed to know why I was there to see Jamie so early or why I went to the tree house instead of their front door.

I climbed the old rungs of the ladder that were bolted into the tree and then reached above me to swing the trapdoor open. Hoisting myself through, I almost fell back to the ground when I was startled by the lone figure that sat against the roughly hewn wall.

Jamie was already in the tree house waiting for me.

CHAPTER FIVE

I looked at him, stunned that he had beaten me to the tree house. He was never anywhere on time, ever. Not only was he on time that day, he was early.

"Jamie, I...."

He put a hand up to stop me, and I climbed all the way through the trapdoor and then sat on the blanket in front of him. He was wearing his typical jeans and screen-print T-shirt that he wore to school every day, but he looked defeated. His black canvas messenger bag was thrown into the corner, and from the way he was sweating, it looked like he'd been in here for a while.

"I'm sorry," he apologized, his face full of remorse, and it broke my heart. Every bit of anger and resentment I had felt over the last twenty-four hours dissipated. I had been an irrational, jealous child, and he needed to know that.

"No, Jamie, I'm sorry," I told him, and his eyes went from the blanket to my face. "I had no right to be jealous. You and I have no kind of commitment." As I spoke, I could feel the anger and resentment start to rise again. "To be honest, I think it was that you were flirting with a girl. It made me think that maybe you weren't... that you weren't being honest with me about... well, about the way you said you felt about me." I felt a familiar burning in my throat, but this time I ignored it.

"That's just it, Brian, I don't like her," he said, and it was my turn to be surprised. "Well, she's nice and all, but I don't like her like that."

"But then why...."

"I heard a few of the girls, including Karen, talking about how much time we spent together, how close we are, how comfortable we are with each other. One of them was talking about how you ran out of the gym when you saw me. Apparently, her brother told her. I overheard Karen telling Emma that maybe I don't like her because I was... well, because I didn't like girls. It scared me, and I wanted to do something to prove them wrong before rumors started to spread. You know how girls are."

I nodded, and guilt gnawed at my stomach. He had done it to protect us. He was pretending to like a girl, forcing himself into that mold for us, and I had run away like a child.

"I'm so sorry; I should have asked, given you a chance to tell me," I started, but again he cut me off.

"No, I should have told you about the girls talking. I had planned to when you stayed over Saturday night, but we kind of got... distracted. Knowing that I would see them in church on Sunday, I'd been planning to flirt a little with Emma to shut them up. I meant to tell you. It made me so upset to know that I had hurt you." Turning around quickly on the blanket, he sat beside me and held my hand. "There are so many ways that this could go wrong, and I'm scared every day, but I don't want you to ever think that I don't think what we have is worth every bit of it." Lifting his hand, he caressed my face. I would never get tired of feeling his skin against mine as he touched me.

I wrapped my arms around his neck, elated by his admission. Sitting there in the sweltering heat of the early morning sun filtering through the open window, we held each other. Everything in our relationship was uncertain, except how we felt about each other.

I promised myself that I would never doubt his feelings for me again.

We got to school just in time to make it to first period. Talking and kissing in the tree house, we had almost forgotten we were supposed to go to school. Sliding into our seats just as the bell rang, we grabbed our books from our bags and faced the front when the teacher entered.

That was when Jamie got the note.

The note was passed from teenager to teenager through the line behind him and tossed over his shoulder by an excited-looking Gina Trammel. A curly redhead from the same group of friends as Karen and Emma, she watched eagerly as Jamie opened the folded projectile under his desk. Following the obvious path the note had taken, my eyes landed on Karen. She was practically bouncing in her chair, her eyes lit with excitement. An embarrassed-looking Emma sat next to her, trying to make herself disappear as she scooted lower and lower behind her institutional desk.

Glancing over at Jamie, I saw that he had a small smirk, and his face was flushed from his neck to his ears to his forehead. The change in color was subtle, but having spent so much time looking at him, I could tell the difference. While the teacher wrote notes on literary irony, Jamie did some writing of his own and then sent the note back through the winding path of students to its originator.

Karen's face lit up like she had just won the lottery, and she leaned over to relay whatever Jamie had written. At first Emma's face went blank with shock, and then it blossomed into a tentative smile. Her face held a dreamy expression through the rest of the lecture. When I glanced at Jamie, all I could garner from his expression was self-satisfaction.

Finally, after an excruciating hour of discussing stuff we were never going to use again as long as we lived, the bell rang, and we were free. I packed up quickly and waited for Jamie. Before he threw his backpack over his shoulder, he looked back at Emma and winked. Her face went scarlet, and she made a beeline for the door. The rest of the students soon followed, but I grabbed Jamie's arm before he could tag along with the group.

"Okay, spill," I said, not in the mood to be coy.

"We have a double date Friday night," he said without missing a beat. I raised my eyebrows incredulously. Karen was all right to hang out with, I guess, but to actively date her? I wasn't sure I could keep up that kind of facade; I barely even knew her.

"What if, after spending time alone with us, they figure out that we're more into each other than we are into them?" I whispered, and he turned to me, paling slightly.

"I hadn't thought of that. I just thought it was the perfect cover," he said, and I could see his mind going over all of the different possibilities, the varied outcomes of the night. "I think we'll be all right. I mean, it's only going to be a movie or whatever. We can handle it, and it will help solidify our cover."

"What if she wants you to kiss her at the end of the night?" I asked, maybe a little louder than I'd meant to. Our teacher looked up and shooed us off to our next class. After heading up the hall we ducked into the boys' bathroom to continue our conversation. Jamie checked the stalls to make sure we were alone.

"I will tell her that kissing is important to me, and not something I take lightly," he shrugged. "That's actually true, too, so it's not like I'm lying to the girl. You are the first person I have ever kissed, and that meant everything to me." I nodded as the door opened and a senior I recognized faintly from the wrestling team entered. Jamie started to wash his hands, and I followed his example. Then we picked up our bags and headed for class.

The rest of the week was a blur of classes and assignments as we waited with sick fascination for Friday to arrive. I'd cleared the date with the Schreibers, Richard giving me a couple of twenties to pay for the evening's activities. I think he and Carolyn were pleased that I was trying to be a normal teenager. They had been whispering lately about whether my "trauma" was affecting my social development, since I was almost seventeen and had never been on a date. The first time I'd heard them talking in hushed whispers from the living room, I'd nearly laughed out loud. I was glad that they cared so much about how I was doing, but they were just so far off base. If it hadn't been so serious, it would have been funny.

Jamie's parents were delighted that he was taking Emma on a date. He could have done worse, could have chosen a girl with "loose morals," but they knew their boy had a good head on his shoulders and would never pick a girl like that. I hoped that neither Jamie nor I would ever have to find out what they would say if they knew that it wasn't the nice girl Jamie had chosen, but the poor throwaway boy from a few streets over.

Every boy must wonder what his first date will be like. *Will it be with a cheerleader or the cute girl in math? Will we go to dinner or a movie? Perhaps break with tradition and go on a picnic, or stick with the local mini-golf course?* A few times, even against my own internal, feeble protests, my mind strayed to Jamie and me at the beach, or on a walk through the woods near our houses. Never in my wildest imagination did I come up with the reality of Friday night.

What I wanted more than anything was to go to the movies alone with Jamie. I wanted for us to be free to hold hands or even make out like any other couple would. I wanted for us to go to the local pizza place and talk about our future together over a small pepperoni and a couple of drinks. Unfortunately, that wasn't meant to be, not with the two silly, giggling girls who would soon be lodged between us.

Since Jamie was the only one with a license, it was up to him to drive us into the scenic town of Jackson Creek. Our parents would never let us go all the way to Mobile alone, so Jackson Creek was it. The town contained exactly one movie theater and three restaurants, which was more than our own tiny hometown of Crayford. Richard had once told me that our town had gotten its name because a clerk in the early 1800s was transcribing documents and miscopied the W in Crawford as a Y. Now we have to explain, and spell slowly, the name of Crayford for eternity, and we have no real place for a teenager to hang out on Friday night.

Jamie picked me up first for our little adventure, and my heart thudded in my chest as we held hands for the short drive. They lay clasped between us on the unused emergency brake, our hands fitting together so naturally. Looking over at me as we pulled onto Oak Street, just a block from Karen Simmons's pink flamingo-decorated house, he squeezed my hand and said, "I wish it were just us tonight." Then he sighed, and I looked over to see that we were in front of the house.

To say that the yard was infested with lawn ornaments was really not doing justice to the Simmons's creative Mecca. Practically every square inch of the weathered ground was covered with lounging flamingos, dancing mice, and the occasional fountain. Outsiders might have mistaken it for a yard sale, except there was no such sign. The only reason I could think of for having such adornments was to detract from the rundown house. Maybe if your eyes were drawn to the giant inflatable Disney characters, you wouldn't notice the missing shutters or the plastic sheeting covering the poorly insulated windows.

Glancing at Jamie again, I noticed that his posture was stiff. He wasn't looking forward to this any more than I was, but it was necessary. I had to keep him safe, and if that meant enduring a date with Karen Simmons, it was what I'd have to do. So I kept putting one foot in front of the other until we were at the door.

Mr. Simmons opened the door and, with a rather somber expression, invited us in. He greeted Jamie like a long-lost son, but my reception was much cooler. Chalking it up to the fact that I was the one taking his daughter out, I ignored him. When the girls finally came downstairs, Karen was wearing a brand new sundress, probably purchased specifically for this occasion. She was decked out with a little of what I guessed was her mother's makeup and a lot of perfume. It was everything I could do not to take a step back as she bounded over next to me.

Emma was altogether different. She wore a pink sweater and jeans, looking much more comfortable than any of us felt. Forgoing makeup, her hair was swept up off of her face into a twist at her neck. It suited her. She looked sweet but almost stylish and had thankfully skipped the cologne.

As we started to walk out the door, we got the obligatory speech about taking care of the girls. Then her dad went on again about being a gentleman with his daughter. To be honest, I had tuned him out, because really, he had nothing to worry about. I glanced over at Jamie to see if he thought the speech was as amusing as I did and was startled to see that he was angry. More than angry, he was enraged. Emma and Karen must have noticed too, because they started pulling us out the door. Karen tossed a quick comment saying, "Daddy, we're going to be late!" over her shoulder just before she hastily pushed Emma though the door, letting it slam shut behind her.

I noticed as we opened the passenger doors for the girls that Jamie's hands were shaking. The girls climbed in quickly, and after we shut the doors, Jamie with a little more force than necessary, I followed him around to the other side of the car. Laying my hand on his shoulder, I asked him what had upset him. He sighed and opened the door, shaking his head. Taking that to mean "not now," I followed his lead and climbed into the back seat next to Karen, who looked almost ashamed.

"Apparently, old man Simmons doesn't think that some common foster kid is good enough for his precious little girl," Jamie said, his voice teeming with scathing disapproval. Karen sat forward and put her hands on the back of Emma's seat. It looked as though she was going to apologize for her father, until Jamie punctuated his remarks by calling him a "fucking prick." Emma's hand flew over her mouth, and Karen gasped.

"Jamie," I said, putting my hand on his shoulder again. "It's not important. Let's just go have a good time."

Of course, it felt important. While we were in the house, I pretty much ignored the guy because I thought he was just going through the normal fatherly bullshit. Not until Jamie got so upset about it did I realize what the man didn't like was me. It felt like someone had poured peroxide on the searing hole inside me caused by my parents' deaths. The sting, the pain, brought with it a hard lump in my throat. Yes, I was an orphan, a burden on the Schreibers; no one knew that better than I did. To say that I wasn't good enough for his little Karen was ludicrous, but what stuck with me was the question of whether or not I was good enough for Jamie.

I sat back against the seat, contemplating. Jamie noticed, and I saw the physical effort he was making not to reach back and comfort me. His hands danced on the steering wheel, his shoulders were taut, and his eyes darted back to mine in the mirror every few seconds. However, before either of the girls could notice, Karen spoke up in her father's defense, and then the shouting started. Watching it, dazed, it felt like some kind of perverted tennis match. The shouting volleyed back and forth between Jamie and Karen as Emma held her hands over her ears and I watched in fascination. Then, to my astonishment, when Karen began to attack Jamie's character, Emma pulled her hands down.

"Stop it!" Emma yelled deafeningly in the small confines of the Mayfield's old Ford Taurus. "Just stop, Karen. What your father said was out of line, period. Brian is a good guy. Jamie, Karen's father might be a bigot, but he was just looking out for his daughter's welfare. Can we please go now?" Her breathing was quick and shallow; her brunette curls had started to fall haphazardly from the twist. As Jamie started the car, she reached up and pulled her hair down, allowing it to fall in waves over her tensed shoulders. Karen sat back against the seat, clearly stunned by her wallflower friend's outburst.

The rest of the evening was relatively uneventful after its tumultuous beginning. Following a few mumbled comments of "I don't care" or "whatever you want to see" at the theater, we decided on a comedy. After the debacle the night had become, we needed a few laughs. The girls sat in the middle, popcorn ready, flanked by Jamie and me on either side.

By the time the evening was over, I was exhausted just from keeping up the pretense. I was sick of pretending that I wanted to be with these girls; I was sick of pretending that Karen wasn't obnoxious; and mostly, I was sick of having to stop myself from showing affection for the boy that I cared so much about. Thankfully, Jamie and Emma started laughing and talking halfway through the movie, making things marginally less awkward. It seemed that they had a lot in common. Karen and I didn't feel the need to speak. It was easier to avoid talking in the theater, but the car ride home was just uncomfortable.

After walking the girls up to the door and saying a quick goodnight, we couldn't get to the car fast enough. We had close to an hour left before we had to be home, and we planned to spend it alone.

CHAPTER SIX

Over the course of the next few weeks, Jamie and I talked at length about Emma. Together we decided that Jamie should keep up the pretense of dating her. It was nauseating to watch them together, and there was certainly ample opportunity to do so, because it seemed, to me at least, that they were always together. They sat together at lunch amidst our group of friends; she came over after school so they could work on their history project; he even walked her to school because she lived right up the street. As Jamie was a constant in my day, she became a constant in his.

I hated to sound so petty about it, but it bothered me that the time he spent with her cut into the time he and I got to spend together. Thankfully, this week was the last week of school. Maybe once we were on summer vacation, Jamie and I could spend some quality time together. Again, I thought about afternoons at the beach or walking through the woods where no one could see. With only one more year of high school, I wanted us to start making decisions about what we were going to do the next year. I had already started writing essays for college scholarships, praying that I could get into whatever colleges to which Jamie planned to apply.

Much to my annoyance, it seemed that Emma had been thinking about it as well. She and her friends talked at lunch like Emma and Jamie were already engaged or something.

"Have you started thinking about colleges, Em?" Karen asked from Emma's other side. This had been a subject I'd heard from many of our classmates frequently over the past few weeks. We were now racing toward our senior year, and it was time to start making plans for the future. If my childhood hadn't been so goddamned awful, I'd lament becoming an adult.

"I have been, but Jamie and I haven't really talked about it yet," Emma said with a shrug, and Jamie nearly spewed his milk over my lunch tray. She gave him a raised eyebrow look, the one Carolyn used with Richard if he contradicted her. Only while Carolyn's look was generally amused, Emma's look was anything but.

I had no doubt that Jamie would hear about that later.

While it was the last week of school, it was probably the one that tried my patience the most. On Monday, Emma helped Jamie on the facial structure of his drawing, smoothing out the rough edges and softening the lines. Had I not been so preoccupied with the way her hands lingered on his shoulders, I'd have seen that the drawing looked remarkably like me. On Tuesday, I had to watch Jamie's hands holding Emma's as she steadied her piece of plywood on the shop house saw. He was showing her how to make the cuts perfectly even in order to finish her project.

On Thursday, he got to be her counselor.

"Hey, are you okay, Emma?" Jamie asked in a low voice while the others were still in line for their mystery meat. Since Jamie, Emma, and I all had geography together, we were just down the hall and usually arrived first. I pretended to be really interested in the grayish lump on my tray as Emma looked up at Jamie. She did look rather upset, I saw from my quick sideways glance.

"My brother's girlfriend broke up with him after practice last night, and he's really upset about it," she said with a sigh. Emma's fraternal twin, Brad Mosely, was one of our school's best pitchers. "She said that she was dumping him for Tim Deans, that new kid from Ohio. He wasted a whole year on her. I think he really thought it was going somewhere, and that's what bothers him most." Emma pushed her tray away, just keeping her apple juice.

"It just makes me so angry that she would treat him that way," she continued. "I'd love nothing more than to walk up to her in gym later and smack her senseless." At that, I had to look up. I'd never heard meek little Emma talk about hitting anyone.

"You and Brad must be very close," I commented, not sure if I was supposed to even be part of this conversation. She seemed to tolerate me because I was Jamie's best friend, but I got the feeling that she was jealous of our closeness. He said that once, she'd even said that maybe I should be his girlfriend. That sent him into a little bit of a panic until I assured him that I didn't think she meant it quite that way.

"He's my twin brother, technically my big brother by two and a half minutes. He means the world to me, and it just makes me so mad that he's hurting."

The constant interaction between Emma and Jamie continued throughout the day, until I sat conspicuously alone in study hall.

I checked around to make sure I hadn't missed him when I had come in, but he wasn't there. Neither was Emma. *Had they gotten sick? Was Jamie hurt and was she helping him?* Jamie never ditched, and hard as it was for me to admit, Emma wasn't that kind of girl. No one else in the class seemed to have noticed their absence. Even Karen was just leafing through some teenage magazine, passing the time until the period was over. I left the dingy paperback I had been reading on my chair as I walked up to the teacher's desk.

"Mrs. Barachek, I had to stay late in my last class and didn't get a chance to use the rest room on my way here. May I please have the pass?" I asked in an angelic voice. Mrs. Barachek, the matronly lady who also ran the lunch line, knew I was a good student. The faint smell of cabbage accompanied the pass that she handed to me without a word. I left the classroom and turned right, toward the bathroom, just in case she was watching.

Looking up and down each hallway, I started to panic when I couldn't find him. *Had he been beaten up? Where the hell was he?* Frantically, I ran down the south hallway and skidded to a stop when I heard his voice. He was talking, but I couldn't make out what he was saying, and then everything went quiet. I sprinted down the hall and quietly opened the band room double doors at the end. If he was talking to a teacher, I didn't want to get either of us into trouble. I just needed to know that he was okay.

The sight of Jamie kissing Emma as she sat on the teacher's desk and he stood in front of her nearly brought me to my knees. My eyes caught every detail, from her hands on the outsides of his thighs to his fingers in her hair. It seemed like time stood still for just an instant before they realized that I was there. My chest ached, and I heard a faint ringing in my ears as finally, mercifully, they broke apart. Jamie's eyes met mine, and he looked like someone who had been caught with his hand in the cookie jar. The door banged on the wall with the force of my anger, and the panic that replaced the guilt in Jamie's face went unnoticed by Emma, who was still smiling dreamily. Her eyes were closed and her mouth slightly open, just waiting for her prince to continue the kiss. Backing out of the room, I heard Jamie call out after me, but I didn't stop. I turned and ran. It was something I had started to become very good at, because I had learned all of my life to avoid conflict.

Thankful that Carolyn wasn't home when I got there, I kept running until I reached my bedroom. Then, with as much force as I could muster, I slammed my bedroom door. Before I could even reach my bed, the tears had started. I hadn't cried in a long time. When you're in the state home for boys, crying only makes you look weak. Weak kids are easier to pick off.

Lying down with my face buried in the pillow, I let it all out. I let out the frustration of not being able to openly love whomever I wanted, of the pretenses and the lies, of the hiding and the shame, and finally of it not being me that Jamie was kissing in that fucking room.

I must have fallen asleep, because sometime later, as the light was dimming in my room, I heard a distant pounding. Not caring at all what the source of the noise was, I rolled back over and slept. For the first time in a long time, I didn't have any dreams. It seemed that my body and my mind were too exhausted to come up with anything to reveal to me or even torture me with through a dream. For the uninterrupted rest, I was grateful.

When my alarm went off the next morning, I had absolutely no intention of getting out of bed. It was Friday, and the last day of the school year. Turning it off, I rolled over and stared out of the window. After about half an hour, Carolyn came up to my room to check on me.

"You're going to be late, darlin'," she said from the doorway, only halfheartedly. Since I hadn't been out of my room since I'd gotten home from school the day before, I'm sure she had figured out that something was wrong. I remembered at some point during the evening hearing my bedroom door open and close. Obviously, she had come to call me for dinner, but since I had been sleeping, she had decided to let me rest.

"Carolyn, I haven't missed a day of school all year, and I'm really not feeling all that well. I'd really like to stay home," I said, rolling back over to face her. She came into the room and sat down on my bed. Her touch was gentle and caring as she put her hand on my forehead.

"Boy, you are burnin' up," she said with a small wink. "I'm going to have to call the school and let them know that you won't be in. Do you have anything you need to do today at school, any tests or papers due?"

"No, ma'am, nothing, and I cleaned out my locker the other day. There's just some books in it. I can stop by on Monday and pick them up." She nodded and brushed my curls out of my eyes.

"Then you just stay up here and rest. I'll bring some sandwiches up later." She stood up and walked to the door.

"Thank you, Carolyn," I told her. The gratitude in my voice was unmistakable. The last place I wanted to be was at school. Even though I knew it was part of the grand scheme of things, I didn't want to face Jamie and Emma. I just wanted to lie in bed and imagine a world where Jamie and I could be together.

As promised, around noon Carolyn brought up a couple of sandwiches for me, and I devoured them. Having missed supper the night before, I was ravenous when she set them in front of me. Two creamy peanut butter and apple jelly sandwiches and a huge glass of milk improved my outlook on the day. Grabbing a paperback book from my shelf, I spent the rest of the afternoon reading on my bed. By the time I had finished the first quarter of the book, I was dozing lightly in the mid-afternoon sun.

When I woke, Jamie was sitting on the end of my bed.

Sitting up, I quickly set the book on my bedside table and then adjusted my blankets, not looking at him. It was an effort to contain the hurt and the sense of loss that I felt because he was in the room with me. The whole incident had become fairly abstract overnight, but with him sitting there, the realization and the memory came forcefully home. When I finally met his eyes, I noticed that they were shadowed and a little bloodshot.

"You know why I have to do this," he said, and the twinge of condescension in his voice made the bile rise in my throat. Of course I fucking knew why he had to do it, why he needed to make out with little Suzy Geek in the band room: because I had a cock. That didn't make it any fucking easier, and that was exactly what I told him.

"Maybe you'll just decide that it's easier to be with her," I commented, tracing the geometric pattern on my sheets with my index finger. "She's the right gender, has the right family, goes to the right church, and apparently has the right lips."

"You're right; it would be easier to be with her. There's one major flaw in that plan however," he said, pausing for just a second as he grabbed my hand. My heart nearly stopped as I waited for him to tell me the argument that would cause it to start beating again. "She's not the one that I'm in love with." My eyes met his as I realized the full impact of his admission. *He was in love with me.* Jamie had just told me that he loved me. For a long moment, I looked into his face, too shocked to speak, not even daring to breathe. But I found my voice.

"What?"

"I love you, Brian. The look on your face when you saw me with her, that horrible shocked, devastated look... it broke my heart. I almost told her then that it was over, but it wouldn't have done either of us any good. She was already starting to get suspicious. That would have just sealed it for her."

I wanted to tell him it didn't matter, that we couldn't be together anyway. We'd always have to hide, and he'd always have to lie and live in fear with me. I wanted to tell him that maybe it wasn't worth it, that we couldn't possibly hold this together. But I couldn't, because it would have been a lie.

"I love you too, Jamie." I had for what felt like my whole life, because really, my life hadn't started until I came to the Schreibers. Although we had grown up together and shared the love of friends, it had grown into something more, something so much stronger. I leaned forward, wishing nothing more than to seal the momentous occasion with a kiss, but it occurred to me that I hadn't brushed my teeth since the day before. Just before our lips met, I clamped my hand over my mouth and jumped off the bed. Brushing my teeth and hair quickly in the bathroom across the hall, I returned within minutes to find Jamie absolutely cracking up on my bed.

"I thought you were going to be sick for a minute," he laughed, trying to catch his breath. "Then I hear the water and the sounds of you brushing your teeth. So much for the perfect moment." As I sat on the bed next to him, he leaned forward and captured my lips with his own. We weren't wound around each other like we normally were when we kissed for the physical pleasure of it. The feeling of his hand wrapped around mine, that simple innocent gesture, was so perfect. Soft, tender kisses chased one another as we moved closer to each other, reveling in our closeness.

It wasn't about sex.

It was about love.

CHAPTER SEVEN

"**B**rian, I'm not sure this is such a good idea," Jamie whispered as we climbed the stairs, walking right past my bedroom to Richard's study. I could feel his hand sweating in mine as I held it. It was one of the few times that we were able to get away with that kind of affection because Richard and Carolyn weren't home. Carolyn was likely out socializing like a good doctor's wife, and Richard was at work. We wouldn't have much time alone, but it would be enough.

"This was your idea, Jamie," I told him, laughing quietly as I pushed open the door and walked over to the computer. Peeking quickly out of the window for cars pulling into the drive, I pulled him closer, down onto the arm of the office chair, and wrapped one arm around his hip.

"I know it was, but this is dangerous." Looking down, he put a hand on my shoulder and squeezed. "If anyone walks in...."

"We'll look quickly so you can see what I was talking about, and then we can go study. Besides, it's Wednesday, which means that Carolyn is at her book club. It ends at four, but they always stay talking afterwards. We have at least forty-five minutes or so," I told him, checking the clock and doing the math in my head. He was right, we were taking an awful risk, but I wanted to turn him on and make him happy. There wasn't much at all that I could offer him in our fledgling relationship but fear and uncertainty. We should have a little fun too.

"Fine, show me," he responded with a sigh, but I could see that he wasn't as exasperated as he was trying to project. In fact, his breathing had picked up slightly in anticipation, and his fingers had tightened a bit on my shoulder. I turned to the computer and hit the power button, waiting for it to load. Jamie didn't look at me; he just kept watching the screen, almost as if something were going to come out of it and bite him. After a few minutes, I clicked past the login, which had no password, and brought up an Internet browser. Using the same reasoning that I had before, I typed in the phrase "gay men" and hit enter. As it had before, the results list showed over fifty-five million entries. One of the first entries was titled "Racing Hearts Studios: a subsidiary of Hartley Entertainment."

I clicked the link and heard Jamie suck in a breath.

The initial screen was enticing, with mostly naked boys frozen in silent laughter or an impassioned kiss. The buttons at the bottom of the site, the ones that made me promise I was eighteen, gave me a very simple choice: enter or leave. Of course, the choice wasn't that simple. Now that I saw the warning, which I must have missed on the last site, I wasn't sure this was a good idea anymore. Praying that what we were about to do wasn't illegal, I glanced nervously at Jamie, who nodded in encouragement, and I clicked the enter button. When the new screen came up and I saw what it was, I immediately clicked minimize and looked out the window to make sure no one could see. The entire middle of the screen was dominated by a video player showing guys having sex. From the second that we'd seen, they were having oral sex, and even through my embarrassment, I was starting to get hard.

Taking one final look back over my shoulder at the door, I clicked the minimized window to bring it back up. The video had ended, but there were dozens of images all over the screen. Even the background image had a guy smiling with his jeans around his knees and his erection in his hand. Taking my hand off of the mouse, I just stared, forgetting even to check the window and the door again for my foster parents, unable to believe what we were looking at.

Near the middle of the screen, I saw another video waiting to be played. The image was of the blond boy I'd seen before who looked so much like Jamie. He was lying back on a patio lounger, the blue and white striped chair contrasting with his perfectly tanned skin. A small, sheepish smile played at the corners of his lips as his hand rested on the lower part of his stomach just under his hard cock. Without seeking permission from Jamie, without making sure it was safe, without even breathing, I clicked play. A long sequence of white titles and yellow names scrolled across the brilliantly green little screen until nearly half of the progress bar had elapsed.

When he appeared on the screen, his eyes were closed and he had both hands between his legs. My hand gripped the mouse convulsively to stop myself from rubbing my own crotch as the boy on the screen stroked his cock while he rubbed his balls. His quiet moans drifted through the small speakers on the desk, and I finally checked the door and the window to make sure we wouldn't be walked in on. Listening to the sounds of that beautiful boy made me feel so guilty, but didn't dampen my excitement.

Movement next to me caught my attention, and my heart pounded as I saw Jamie adjusting himself, his eyes glued to the screen. My breath caught in my throat as his tongue darted out to moisten his full pink lips. A bead of sweat rolled down my temple in the mid-afternoon heat of the room, and I forced my attention away from Jamie and back on the screen. As I did, the scene changed, and the boy was now kneeling on the chair with his back to the camera. Bent a bit at the waist, he was looking back over his shoulder at the camera as he stroked his cock.

I nearly came in my shorts.

"I don't think we should watch this any—" Jamie whispered, but then stopped abruptly, his hand trembling as he pointed at the screen. "Click on that one." I looked to where he was pointing and saw the boy that we had just been watching behind another boy who had shaggy light-brown curls like mine. Sliding the mouse over the pad until the cursor rested on top of the brunette's head, I asked Jamie if he was sure.

"It feels so wrong to be watching, because pornography is the work of the devil. Since we're going to hell for being gay anyway, I want to see." Jamie's reasoning seemed sound enough, even if his voice was shaking as he said it. It wasn't immediately clear if his voice shook because he felt guilty or excited. Turning my face up to him, I grabbed the front of his T-shirt and pulled him down for a quick kiss. My elbow accidentally grazed his cock, which bulged against the straining zipper of his jeans, and he hissed.

Checking the window one more time, I clicked on the video to start the clip.

The boy on his hands and knees was panting in loud, mewling cries punctuated by slaps of skin as the other boy slammed his hips into him. As we watched, the brunette reached underneath his body to stroke his cock just as the camera angle changed. The condom-sheathed dick of the blond was quickly sliding in and out of the other boy's ass. Everything was lewdly visible to anyone who happened to be watching. The boy in back grabbed his partner's hips tightly and slammed harder into him, his breathing choppy and rough from the excitement and exertion.

"You like it?" the blond asked, and the smirk in his voice was unmistakable.

"Yeah, I like it... Harder...," the brunette replied with a grunt as he was taken rougher from behind.

The scene changed again, and the brunette was now on top of the blond, his legs spread as he bounced and stroked himself.

"Turn it off," Jamie choked out and left the room. My cock ached as I scrambled to close the browser. I made sure all of the windows were closed before shutting the computer down and almost running to my room after him.

Just as I came through the door, he caught me in a kiss that would have melted glass.

"Fuck, you make me hard," he murmured against my lips as he reached for the hem of my T-shirt. It took a minute for what Jamie had said to register, our kiss breaking as he whipped my T-shirt off and dropped it on the floor. His lips were back on mine before I could speak, the hunger in his kiss making my heart race. Encouraged by the lust-filled haze my brain seemed to be lost in, I pulled his T-shirt up by sliding my palms under it, feeling his heaving, bare chest. Jamie moaned decadently into my mouth as I grazed my hands over his nipples. When I reached his shoulders, he lifted his arms so that his shirt could join mine on the floor. My arms were around his neck as he started pushing me back toward the bed. I barely had the presence of mind to slam the door with my foot as I stumbled backwards. For the first time, I was thankful that I had a small bedroom, because after just a few steps the backs of my legs hit the bed and he fell on top of me. Our lips never parted as we crawled onto the bed until he cradled his hips between my legs, his chest pressed against mine, our sweat mingling as we held each other, heedless of the heat.

Jamie's hands held my face gently, as if it were precious to him, while I wound my fingers in his hair. Even though my eyes were closed, I could feel that his lips were turned up into a smile, and I smiled too. Rocking my body slowly, my chest rubbed against his, spiraling us to greater heights of arousal. Like a ride at the amusement park, our arousal climbed higher and higher until we reached that peak and then freefell into orgasm.

God, his lips were so soft.

I was panting as he held my knees open with his thighs and rubbed his cock against mine through our thin shorts. Whimpering as I pushed my hips off the bed to get more of the sensation, I buried my face in Jamie's neck, breathing in the scent of sweat and soap. Kissing his neck and shoulder, I felt him plant his hands on either side of my shoulders as his hips moved more insistently. I pulled my knees up, hooking my legs over his, almost wrapping them around his waist.

"Jamie... please...," I moaned against his ear, not knowing what I was begging for exactly, except maybe for him to grind against me like that forever. It felt that good. Listening to make sure I didn't hear anything but our breathing, I reached down and grabbed his ass with both hands while at the same time rolling my hips up. He dropped to his forearms, which he pushed under my shoulders, holding me against his chest. My head fell back against the bed, and he pressed his forehead against my shoulder as we rubbed against each other.

It wasn't romantic and it wasn't sweet. It was pure fucking lust.

"Brian... fuck...," Jamie cried in almost a half sob as his hips jerked faster against me. The need, the vulnerability in his voice, the way the rolls of his hips were punctuated by soft, desperate sounds, caused a sweet tingling in my groin. My grip tightened on his ass, and I bucked my hips up, using my legs to pull him forward, humping myself against his swollen cock. His sweet, openmouthed cries were coming faster as I felt my balls begin to throb.

I panicked a little at what was about to happen, because we'd never made each other come before. The most we'd ever done together was watch each other masturbate and some groping while we were kissing. Humping each other, rutting against each other simulating sex, was something different. As the fire raced through me, I realized that we had passed the point of no return; the roller coaster had crested the top of the hill.

Before I could get out more than a strangled "Baby," my body locked and my back arched. My hands still gripped his ass as my cock erupted, coating the inside of my briefs with come. It was far more intense than anything I had done with my own hand. His weight on top of me was comforting as I shivered, sliding my hands up his back, holding him as he continued to move his hips against me, trying to find his own pleasure. Turning my head slightly, I captured his lips in a slow kiss, lingering as his whimpers touched my lips. His body began to slow, almost as if he were afraid of what was coming, so I rubbed harder against him, desperate to hear as he reached his peak. With his forehead pressed against mine, I could feel his rapid breathing against my face. Jamie was so beautiful, eyes closed, mouth slightly open. I watched and waited as his body began to tense.

I didn't have to wait long.

Jamie jerked his hips against mine once... twice... three times, and then went still with a soft, drawn-out "Oh" in my ear. I held him against me, on top of me, stroking his hair, just trying to be close to him before the world pulled us apart again.

"Oh God, that was good," Jamie whispered and then chuckled. I would have called it a giggle and teased him about it, but I didn't have the strength to move yet. Apparently he did, because he rolled off of me and then right off of the bed.

"Oh my God, are you okay?" I asked, trying to suppress the laughter but failing miserably. Jamie sat up, rubbing his elbow and smiling ruefully.

"Well, that was graceful." Jamie stood up and pulled the front of his shorts away from his body. "Can you grab some boxers for us, and I'll get something to clean up with?" Swinging my legs over the side of the bed, I stood up and felt the rapidly cooling semen sticking my underwear to my skin. Checking my bedroom window to make sure the drive was still empty, I closed the curtains and pulled my shorts and underwear off, looking up as Jamie came back into the room holding a wet towel.

He didn't say anything, but the way he looked at me as I stood naked by my desk made me flush in the warm room. Handing the hot rag to me and apparently noticing that I hadn't grabbed underwear, he went to my dresser and pulled out two pairs. I caught the pair he tossed to me while he put the other one on. Jamie was a bit taller than me but thinner, so the boxers fit him without a problem. He held his hand out to me, and I gave him the rag, which he promptly threw on the floor before taking my hand and leading me back to the bed.

We lay down side by side in the small amount of space that my twin bed afforded, and I rested my head on his chest as he wrapped his arm behind me and stroked my arm with his thumb. It felt nice just to lie there with him, feeling his breath in my hair and listening to his heartbeat. I knew we would have to scramble if we heard one of the cars drive up, but it was worth just spending quiet time with him.

"Thank you for showing me that site," Jamie said quietly and kissed the top of my head. A nice breeze came through the open window, blowing the curtains and cooling our damp, heated skin. The scent of honeysuckle from a nearby tree permeated the air, helping to clear it of the smell of sweat and come.

"You're welcome, though the site that I saw before was only pictures. There were no... uhm... videos," I said, still a little embarrassed by what we'd seen. Still images were one thing, but watching for the first time as guys had sex on screen was something I may have wanted to do alone.

"Do you think it hurts?" Jamie asked in a whisper, and I was kind of glad he couldn't see my face, which was turning pink again.

"I don't know... I think it probably does... at least at first," I stammered. "If it hurt, no one would do it, though, so it must feel good for both of them." Worried a little at his question, I reached down and took the hand that wasn't stroking my arm, holding it loosely in mine. "Jamie... I don't think I'm ready for... for you to... for us to...."

"No, I know. I'm not either, really. The more that we do together, though, things like today, each step brings us closer. I just... I wanted to talk about it... with you. You know?"

"I know," I said, nodding and turning my head to kiss his chest. "I want to talk to you about it too, because I love the things we do together. One day I want to take that step with you, but I want to wait until we're both at least seventeen."

"I think that's a good plan," he replied, still stroking my arm. I ran my hand lightly over his chest, loving the way his bare skin felt under my touch.

"How do you think guys in a relationship decide who is going to... uhm... give and who... receives?" I asked in a heated whisper, almost afraid to ask it out loud, confirming that I didn't know. Receiving sounded like it would be painful, at least at first, having something that big put... up there. The thought of having Jamie inside me like that, though, as close as two people could possibly be, was exciting to me.

"I don't know; I think maybe they try out different things and see what they like. Otherwise, how else would you know?"

I felt his finger under my chin and looked up into his face.

"We will make our own rules and go as slow as we need to. It's not a race. I just want to make you happy, Brian," Jamie whispered before pressing his palm to my cheek and kissing me very gently on the lips.

"I am happy, Jamie."

It had been a couple of weeks since I had stayed over at Jamie's on a Saturday night. It would have looked suspicious for me to stay over every week, especially since he was dating Emma. So when he asked me over, I jumped at the chance. Even if we had to spend the time listening for his parents, at least we would be together without his little girlfriend. We needed it so much, or at least I felt like we did. Before his revelation of telling me he loved me, I had started to feel distanced from him, and I hated it. When I got to Jamie's house early that afternoon, I was rather confused to find him trying to haul the inflatable mattress up the tree house ladder.

"What are you...?" I started, but he stopped me almost at once by jumping down from where he was perched halfway up the ladder, landing with a thud right in front of me.

"Help me get this up there," he said, out of breath from the exertion. I climbed the ladder, throwing my backpack of clothes into a corner as I climbed up through the trapdoor. Then, lying flat on the floor, I reached down through the open door and grabbed the end of the mattress that Jamie was proffering from his position near the bottom of the ladder. Being exceedingly careful not to snag it on anything, I pulled the deflated mattress up through the door. Next, he handed me the pump and then disappeared into the house while I laid the mattress and the pump near the wall.

Then I realized that other items from Jamie's room had somehow found their way into the tree house. His fan stood near one of the open windows, and his radio was on top of a crate. Again, I wondered what the hell was going on. *Were we sleeping up here, or was this just to make things more comfortable when we spent time here?* Whatever the reason, I was thankful for the fan, because even that early in June the heat in the tree house was staggering.

"Brian!" Jamie called up from under the window. I looked out to see him holding a long extension cord. "Catch!" He laughed and tossed one end up toward the window. It took three tries before I finally caught the damn thing and pulled it through into the tree house. Still chuckling at my abysmal attempts, he climbed up and closed the trapdoor behind him. He was in better spirits than I had seen him in a while. Flopping down on the floor next to where I was sitting, he leaned over and kissed me hello. When he pulled away, a brilliant smile lit up his face.

"I talked Mama into letting us camp out in the tree house whenever you stay over this summer," he said, still slightly out of breath. "At first, I didn't think she'd go for it because she thought we'd sneak girls up here." He chortled and said, "As if," and then continued, "I promised her that there wouldn't be any girls, and then told her how much I really missed camping as a family. We haven't gone in forever because her back is so bad. Then I brought up how we should get use out of the tree house before Daddy tears it down. In the end, she said it would be okay."

I couldn't believe it. We would be alone, really alone.

I practically tackled him in a hug.

"Okay, let's get this stuff set up before supper," he said, standing hunched over in the low space. Jamie laid out two open sleeping bags, and we spread out the mattress on top of them and inflated it. Then, while I put the bedding on the mattress, Jamie plugged in the fan and radio. On another crate, he emptied the contents of his school bag: chips, sodas, and a few cupcakes. We had the perfect clubhouse, and it was all ours. It almost felt like we were moving into our own little place.

Everything was set up and ready in time for supper, and it was a beautiful night to sit outside and eat. Mr. Mayfield grilled some burgers while Mrs. Mayfield laid out potato salad, coleslaw, corn on the cob, and watermelon slices on the patio table outside their back door. Jamie must have done quite a number on his mama for her to go all out like that.

We spent the evening sitting on the stylish but comfortable patio chairs, relaxing and talking with Jamie's parents. We didn't want to seem too eager to get up in the tree house, so while Mr. Mayfield told us stories about fishing with his daddy and brothers and Mrs. Mayfield reminisced about camping trips they'd taken as a family, Jamie and I waited.

After the sun had gone down and the supper dishes were cleaned, Jamie and I were able to grab a couple of flashlights and escape to our sanctuary. That tree house felt like a safe harbor surrounded by stormy seas. There were storms at our homes, storms at school; we were surrounded. The tree house was one place where we could be free.

Climbing up the ladder into the dark tree house alone with Jamie made the physical side of our relationship much less abstract. We were finally completely alone. The reality of it made me suddenly nervous. *What did he expect to happen tonight?* I didn't want to disappoint him, but I wasn't sure what I was ready for yet. My apprehension grew with each step I took up the ladder.

When I came through the trapdoor, Jamie was turning on a battery-operated lantern next to the bed. The knowledge that he was getting the bed ready for us made that anxiety in my stomach twist into knots. I was glad that he had already turned on the fan. It wasn't terribly uncomfortable in the small space, but I was starting to sweat. I stood back near the closed door as he tossed his shoes into a corner, took off his shirt, and sat cross-legged on the bed waiting for me.

Going over to the radio, I turned it on, reducing the volume until it was just background noise. Then, still stalling, I took off my shoes and arranged them neatly next to his. Pulling my T-shirt over my head, I folded it neatly and set it on top of my bag. Breathing out a deep breath, I climbed onto the mattress and sat across from him.

"Brian, I...," he started, but then abruptly stopped. He struggled with what he wanted to say, the words getting stuck before they were able to get out. "I just...." He sighed and looked down at the mattress.

"I'm not sure what you're expecting," he continued in a rush, "and I don't want to disappoint you, but I'm not sure I'm ready to... to go all the way."

I laughed; I couldn't help it. His hurt eyes met mine, and I knew he thought I was laughing at him.

"I have been thinking that very same thing ever since we finished the supper dishes," I said and took his hand; he relaxed and looked somewhat relieved. He must have been as worried about disappointing me as I was about him. "We don't have to do anything other than just lie here and talk for a while." Reaching over, I angled the fan so that it blew directly on us, and then I relaxed onto the pillows next to him. Seeing his open arms, I rolled over into them without any hesitation or doubt, resting my head on his warm bare chest.

"Jamie, what are we going to do after graduation? I mean, assuming we survive senior year," I said half-jokingly. I didn't necessarily mean surviving as in living, though if Jamie's parents ever found out about us, that was certainly a consideration. I was really referring to our relationship and if it could survive a whole year of hiding, of lying. We were strong now, but would we stay that way if he had to keep up the charade with Emma?

"Are you still writing those essays?" he asked while stroking my shoulder with his thumb as we lay comfortably in each other's arms. The deep sound of his voice resonated through his chest as he spoke, and I nodded against his warm skin. Jamie had spent so much time in Emma's company lately, I had been able to crank out five more scholarship essays. It seemed like every scholarship a student applied for required some kind of essay, and, of course, they weren't similar topics, so papers couldn't be reused.

"I was also planning to get a job next year." He pulled back to look down at me.

"Where?" he asked, but before I could answer, he continued. "And how are you going to get there or keep up your grades? If your grades slip, you won't be able to get a scholarship." I couldn't help but chuckle. He raised an eyebrow in obvious inquiry.

"Okay, first, you sound just like your mama. Second, I'd planned to head over to the cotton mills first to see if I couldn't get a three-to-eleven shift. I can do homework for an hour or so after my shift. I can also do it in study hall, at lunch, and on weekends. You'll help me with the stuff I need help on. I can't count on scholarships that might not come. I want to go wherever you go, and if I have to work full-time to get there, I will. I'll do whatever it takes," I finished with conviction. Jamie stared at me, and then slowly, he nodded. It must have been evident to him that he wasn't going to change my mind. "Have you thought about where we should go?"

"I think it's going to depend on what we can afford and what we want to study." Kissing the top of my head and pulling me tighter against his chest, he continued. "I'd like to go somewhere more progressive than the University of Alabama, someplace we can be together and not have to worry. I've been thinking of maybe majoring in Engineering, or maybe something at a school like UCLA or SUNY. California and New York City seem like they'd be places where we wouldn't have to be afraid."

"We would still have to be careful that your parents don't find out, or they'll pull the plug on your tuition," I suggested, turning to kiss the soft skin of his chest.

"Nope. I love my parents, but they have nothing to do with my tuition. Mamaw left me some money when she died, and Mama and Daddy put it away for my college. The account is designated for tax purposes as an educational account; it's my money, not theirs." His smile was triumphant, and I couldn't help but feel optimistic about our future together. If we could just get through the next year, we would be fine. We had the beginnings of a plan. We were in love. We were going to be together.

"Have you thought about what you want to study after high school, Brian?" he asked, pushing my hair back away from my face.

"I love to build things, to create something from nothing. I'm not sure I'm good enough at math to go into architecture, but I was thinking along the lines of construction management," I told him with a slight shrug.

"Your math grades are fine, and if you're serious about architecture, we can start looking into what you'll need to get into a good school. We'll have to find one that offers what we both want." Then he got serious again. "I want for us to always be together, Brian. I can't imagine what my life would be like without you in it every day." I nodded, and for the first time I was completely unable to tell him how I felt. If I couldn't tell him, I would show him. Coming up onto my elbow, I lifted my head from his chest and leaned in slowly to kiss him. With my heart pounding out every bit of the emotion that I was feeling, I kissed him again and again. He was everything to me.

Everything.

The kiss, the passion, it was about more than just love. It was about that sexual need, that craving we had for each other. Pushing me back against the pillows, he lay on my chest, one of his legs wrapped around mine. I couldn't think about the heat of the evening or the uncomfortable inflatable mattress beneath us; all I could think about was him. His kisses grew more urgent, and that swoop of excitement in the pit of my stomach intensified. Alone in the tree house, there was nothing to stop us from expressing every single one of the desires that had been building over the past few months. The fantasies that had plagued me about Jamie since I had been old enough to understand what they meant could be realized in our makeshift sanctuary there among the early summer leaves.

Shivering as his lips traveled an indistinct and as of yet uncharted path down my neck, I tried not to pull as I grasped the long, damp hair on the back of Jamie's head. When I felt his warm breath along my chest, my fingers tightened their grip. As his lips closed around my nipple, my back arched and my hips bucked up into his. A strangled sound erupted from me as he sucked and licked the sensitive skin and our hips ground together. Even through the heavy material of our jeans, the friction of his pelvis rubbing desperately against my throbbing erection was enough to bring me to the edge. Thankfully, I was able to hold off, because as he moved lower I felt the whisper of his lips across my stomach.

The hand that was not in his hair then went to his shoulder, not to guide him, but simply for my own selfish comfort. I was both terrified and exhilarated by what was coming; my biggest, most exciting fantasy was about to come true. Chancing a glance down at him just as his mouth covered the area right above my waistband in exquisite, wet kisses, I saw that his eyes were closed but that he had a small, sweet smile on his lips.

Suddenly, he slid his body back up so that it was half on top of mine again, but before I had time to be disappointed, he was kissing me with long, deep, fiery kisses that made me wrap one of my legs around his waist and pull him closer. Slowly he broke the kiss and, after nuzzling his face against my neck, asked in a low, breathless voice, "Can I touch you?"

Without even the briefest hesitation, I nodded, and the word "please" was drawn from me just by the excitement and longing that I heard in his request. A gentle hand brushed over my stomach, and I panicked just a little as I felt his fingers undoing my jeans. My heart rate accelerated wildly, and I grabbed the sheet, balling it up in my fists on either side of my hips. Except for my heavy breaths, I lay paralyzed with him on his side right next to me as his hand slid into my jeans, and he stroked me through my briefs. I was so hard, and it felt so fucking good.

"Let's see if doing my homework pays off," he muttered. Dimly, I remembered the bag he wouldn't let me see at the mall bookstore and wondered what he'd gotten. Quiet mewling sounds were pulled from me at even the idea of what he might have learned.

My whimpers didn't go unnoticed, and he smirked slightly as he traced the contours of my erection though the thin material. I didn't know what to do with my hands, so I fisted the sheet on either side of me, wanting to touch him but feeling incredibly shy about it. It was everything I could do just to keep my eyes on his as he pulled my desperately hard cock free from its trappings. Slowly he broke our gaze and looked down to see me, all of me.

With what seemed like a sudden burst of courage, he slid back down so that his shoulders were level with my hips and began pulling my jeans and briefs down. The suspended realization about what we were doing battled with the love, the excitement that I felt at his touch. I lifted my hips until both pieces of clothing were lying on the mattress at my feet. It felt so strange, yet almost natural, to be lying nude for Jamie with the breeze from the fan blowing over my skin. Taking his time, his eyes traveled over every inch of me, from my feet, up my calves, and over my thighs. He lingered at my hips, lightly stroking me as he took his fill of the sight before him. Then his eyes traveled up my stomach and my chest, finally meeting my own slightly embarrassed gaze.

His body hovering over mine, he kissed me gently. "You are so beautiful," he whispered between sweet romantic kisses. Then once again, he was gone, and the next thing I felt nearly sent me through the roof. It was Jamie's tongue as he licked the underside of my cock. I couldn't watch him anymore, and my head drove back into the pillow as he swirled his tongue over what felt like every inch of me. Soon he was concentrating on just the head, sucking lightly. It was indescribable, like my whole body was on fire and the source was beneath his lips. Nothing had ever felt that good, certainly not my own fumbling hand. His mouth closed around me, and he sucked as he bobbed his head carefully. The knuckles on both of my hands were white with the strain of gripping the sheet as my back arched, and he took me deeper. I heard a muted gagging sound, and he pulled back but didn't let me fall from his lips.

My orgasm was already so close; there was no way I was going to last much longer.

The sounds that were ripped from me were primal, guttural, as the freight train force of my orgasm approached. While I tried desperately not to push my hips up, to push my cock deeper into his mouth, it was a battle that I lost. I felt his fingers tentatively stroking between my legs. I would sometimes touch or pull on my balls as I jacked off, but this was different. It was Jamie. His touch was as unexpected as it was exciting. As his head continued to move, sliding my cock in and out of his mouth as he sucked me, I was forcibly reminded of those pictures on the computer. The memory of the looks of sheer pleasure on those boys' faces made me wonder what my own expression was as I spread my legs further and gave him full access to my body.

When everything started to tighten and that familiar feeling came over me, I froze. I didn't want my semen to go into his mouth; that was just gross, but I wasn't sure if I should say something or if he would already know. Time was rapidly passing; that burning tingle was spreading throughout my body. As the wave started to break over me, I pushed him back, grabbing my cock in my shaking hand. "Move," I panted and felt him put his hand over mine, stroking my cock along with me.

The gesture was so intimate.

I stopped for just a second, splaying my fingers, and he entwined his with my own as I resumed stroking myself. At that moment, what I really wanted was to watch him, but my orgasm exploded through me with such force that my muscles locked and sounds that I had never made before flowed like the tide. Years of masturbating with my foster parents down the hall had taught me to be virtually silent as I came, so the low grunts and cry of his name surprised me as I bucked my hips up, fucking our entwined hands. The feeling was so intense and felt like it could go on for hours. Pressing my knees, already so wide apart, into the mattress, my hips jerked up in rapid, uncontrolled thrusts, and I felt my semen spatter onto my heaving stomach and chest.

Panting, I finally let go of the sheet and put one shaking hand over my eyes. Jamie lay down next to me and grabbed a hand towel that must have been lying next to the mattress. It was amazing how he had planned ahead. He swiped the towel across my stomach and then handed it to me so I could clean my hand. Wrapping his arm around my heaving chest, he rested his head on my shoulder.

"Was that okay?" His question was so timid that I almost didn't hear it over the sound of my own heart pounding in my ears. Using my fingers to lightly tilt his chin up, I looked into his crystal blue eyes to witness his affection and devotion. I kissed Jamie, trying to show him how much what he'd done meant to me. The bond, the connection, I felt with him had just been extraordinarily deepened. I loved him more than I could ever remember loving anyone.

"It was incredible, Jamie. I have never, ever felt like that before." His face brightened, a huge smile spreading across his perfect features. I expected him to look different after what we had just shared, because now I looked at him differently. The term "lover" seemed so inadequate for the beautiful boy lying with me as I pushed his hair, damp with sweat, off of his forehead. He shifted positions slightly, and I felt his hard cock against my thigh, bringing back the reality of what I needed to do.

Being intimate with Jamie didn't seem so intimidating now. He made me feel things I had never experienced, a high that I scarcely knew existed. It occurred to me that he must have been as scared about going down on me as I was about doing it to him. But he had done it because he wanted to show me the depth of his feelings. Jamie had made sure I had felt every bit of his affection, his love for me, as he did something that he was so unsure of. He would have done anything for me, of that I was sure.

It was my turn, and I was ready.

Without pretense or hesitation, I scooted down on the mattress until my face was at his chest. He looked down at me, but before he could argue, I smiled at him and ran my fingers lightly over his nipples. Any protest that he might have offered up died in his throat, and he lay back against the pillows. With nerves much too frayed to try to take things slowly, I nuzzled my face into his stomach. Reaching down, Jamie fingered my damp curls as I tried to unbutton his jeans. They were tighter than mine, and I fumbled uselessly with the button fly. Sighing in frustration, I was surprised when his hands gently moved mine and unbuttoned his fly, and he lifted his hips and pulled his jeans off. I was shocked to find that he wore nothing underneath; the thought was just incredibly hot to me.

His cock stood long and lean and proud as it protruded from his coarse dark blond hair, his small pink sac sitting just below his impressive erection. As I had done, he spread his legs wide and gave me room. It was too dark to see anything with much clarity, but I could see enough. The fear returned in earnest when he was naked and lying in front of me. Not wanting to stop, I wrapped my fingers around his shaft instead, touching him as I would myself. It felt entirely foreign to me, but I dipped my head and kissed his hip. He moaned, squirming on the mattress as I touched him.

"God, Brian, that feels so good." His voice was barely above a whisper, but there was an electric charge, a hunger, in it. I was turning him on, and something stirred in me, something powerful. The love, the desire, the absolute need in his voice, his vulnerability lying naked beneath my touch, it was... it was sexy. I was exciting him, and that made me feel powerful and more in control. He wanted me to make him feel good, to give him pleasure. Looking up, I noticed that his eyes were closed, and he was gripping the sheets just as I had. It didn't take much to remember the way he had made me feel, the force of it, the intensity.

Taking small steps, I continued to pump him as I pressed my lips to his inner thigh, and I'm sure he could feel my breath on the sensitive apex between his legs. As I stroked, my hand twisted lightly over the head of his cock, and I placed another long, wet kiss on his hip, moving farther down between his spread legs. The sounds that he was making, almost piteous whimpers, egged me on further. Taking one more small step, I tentatively kissed his sensitive sac, and he almost whined in response. I grinned, pleased that I could have that kind of effect on him. Emboldened by his response, I gently licked the wrinkled skin. The taste was salty and almost bitter, with a harsh bumpy texture. The hairs tickled my lips as I licked him again, smelling the latent fragrance of his body wash, and he cried out sharply.

"Oh, God," he moaned, and I'm not sure that he even realized that he had spoken. It was apparent that he was incredibly excited by my touch, his whimpers and soft cries strengthening my resolve. My touch. Before I lost my nerve, I ran my tongue slowly from his balls up the underside of his cock, as he had done with me. The response was immediate; his back arched, and his hand moved from the wadded sheet to my hair. That small token of affection bolstered my confidence, because no matter what else happened, whether I was good or not, he would love me.

Taking a deep breath, I wrapped my lips around his beautiful cock.

His fingers tightened in my hair, and I continued to caress him with my hand while I sucked on the head. Salty precome mixed with my saliva as my lips slid effortlessly over his smooth skin. Unable to think of anything else to do, I traced the ridges of the head with my tongue. He threaded his fingers through my hair as his other hand stroked my cheek; I laid my other hand on his hip, my thumb affectionately rubbing it in slow, lazy circles. I tried to remember what he had done earlier for me, and again I wondered at what his homework had consisted of. I could have used a little of that reading material. The image of his bobbing head came to mind, and I decided to try that. Holding the base of his cock steady with my hand, I bobbed my head, letting my lips rub over his skin.

"Oh yeah...." I moved my head faster, occasionally grazing his cock with my teeth by accident. Jamie either didn't notice or didn't care. Squirming against the mattress, it seemed that he was having the same trouble I'd had, trying hard not to thrust up into my mouth. My jaw started to ache from the strain, but I continued to suck him. His breathing became labored, and his legs trembled faintly.

"Please...," he whispered, although I had no idea what he was begging for. I was about to pull back and ask him when his fingers tightened almost painfully in my hair. "Brian... Jesus...," he cried, and I sucked harder, wanting to hear him call my name again. When I felt his muscles tightening under my fingers, it occurred to me why he must have called my name. It wasn't an impassioned cry, but a warning. I pulled back just in time for his cock to erupt on my cheek and then his stomach. Ignoring the wetness on my face, I continued to touch him with my hand, his semen making my hand glide effortlessly over his heated skin. I kept stroking even after his cock had stopped jettisoning the white, sticky splotches over his skin. After a moment, he pulled his hips back into the mattress out of my grasp, begging me to stop because the sensation was too much.

Picking up the towel that he had discarded next to the bed, I wiped my face and then his stomach. I laid my head gently against the soft skin of his stomach. Feeling him run his fingers absently through my hair, I wrapped an arm tentatively around his hips, completely unable to believe what I had just done. His hand moved down to run lightly over my back. In the afterglow, I felt so content. Of course we were meant to be together. Tonight had just proven it. We fit together so easily, knew instinctively what brought each other pleasure.

"Brian," Jamie began. Sitting up slightly, I turned to look at him. He was smiling slightly, and his expression was full of hope, of promise. In that moment I could see my whole future, just lying here beside me on this worn, inflatable mattress. "I love you." Kissing his hip once, I crawled back up the mattress until we were level and wrapped both of my arms around him. He sighed, a very contented sound, and with one arm around me, he put his other hand on my face, cupping my cheek. I leaned into his palm and then said the most important words of my young life. Even though I'd said them before, they meant so much more to me after the intimacy that we had just shared.

"I love you too, Jamie."

After getting dressed, we lay in each other's arms, talking late into the night. I knew we had to get up for church the next morning, but it had been so long since we could just be together alone. Jamie rested his head on my chest, and I played with his hair as he ran his fingers over my stomach. We talked about things we'd like to do before the summer was over, and we talked again about what we would do once we had graduated. It all hinged on what we could afford and where we could feel safe being together.

When we were on the verge of sleep, it occurred to me that I was lying alone with Jamie, our limbs entwined comfortably, after the best orgasm I had ever had. I never, ever thought we would be where we were right then. As his breathing evened out, I wished I could freeze that moment in time.

It was like being in heaven.

The scream wakes him up.

It sounded like Mommy, and it wasn't far away. Just the thought that something had made Mommy scream like that causes his small heart to pound in his chest. The little boy scoots down in his big boy bed, his spaceman pajamas riding slightly up his back. He crawls around the plastic railing that Mommy and Daddy put in place to keep him from falling out of bed because they love him. His feet make no noise on the carpeting as he creeps to his bedroom door. The muffled argument coming from the living room is nearly overpowered by his loud and frantic breathing. The door has been left open a few inches in case the monsters come out from under the bed.

Peeking around the doorjamb, he looks first to the right, toward his parents' bedroom, but sees nothing. Then he looks to the left, toward the living room, and sees shadows dancing on the wall. They twist and stretch in the diffused light, looking frightening. Gripping the doorknob tightly in his little fist, he watches, his tiny bare feet frozen where the blue carpeting of his room turns into the light carpeting that runs through the rest of the house.

His mother screams again, and a crash reverberates down the darkened hall. The scream tears right through the terrified little boy, ripping away any lingering thoughts of safety or comfort. Why was Mommy screaming? Where was Daddy? He wants his mother. He wants to be brave and help her, but if it's too big for Mommy, then it's too big for him too. Big boys don't cry, so he wipes away his tears.

Two loud noises crack the very air around him. They sound like fireworks, only much closer and much louder. A warm wetness spreads through his big boy diaper. He runs back to his bed, heedless of the noise his feet make, and hides under the blankets. His only thought is that Mommy or Daddy will come soon. They have to come soon. Please, please let them come soon.

The house is silent, and the boy waits.

He doesn't hear any more crashes, or bangs, or screams. Whatever was making Mommy scream must be gone. Impatient as any young boy, it doesn't take long for him to crawl out of the warm safety of his bed. Again there is no sound as he creeps carefully to his bedroom door. His heart starts another wild gallop as he sticks his head out. He sees that there are no more shadows on the wall and begins to breathe a little slower. Everything is still, and the quiet presses on his tiny ears. He needs to be a big boy now, a big brave boy.

Taking a deep breath just like they do on TV when they're scared, he walks slowly down the hall. His little hand trembles slightly as it glides over the bumpy surface of the wall and he gets as close to it as he can. Even though he's small for his age, he tries desperately to make himself even smaller. Finally, the hallway opens onto the living room, and he takes his first step inside. The boy is shocked to see that the room is in shambles. The TV is gone, the radio is gone, the front door is open, and his parents are lying on the floor. The boy runs to his mother and tries to wake her. Her limbs loll uselessly as he shakes her, which frightens him. He doesn't understand why her eyes are open but she doesn't wake up. The blood seeping from the hole in her chest makes him wonder if she fell down.

He doesn't know what to do; it looks like Daddy is sleeping too.

He wants to run, to hide, to find someone to help, but he can't bring himself to leave his mother.

Finally, the little boy sits on the floor next to his mother and takes her cool hand into his, like she always does when he's scared.

"It will be okay, Mommy," he whispers softly as he squeezes her big hand with his.

Then he watches out the front door for the monster to return for him, and he waits.

I woke with a start, not sure what had interrupted the strange dream I'd been having, but immediately I was unnerved. Jamie sat up beside me, and when he put his hand on mine, I relaxed.

"Brian, you're in the tree house, it's okay. You're safe," he reassured me, no doubt remembering the first few nights I had stayed over with him when we were younger. I had screamed loud enough to wake the whole neighborhood, terrifying not only Jamie but his parents as well. Mrs. Mayfield had called Richard and Carolyn, who had immediately come over to calm me. After the first night, Jamie's mama had told him she didn't think it was a good idea for me to stay again, but Jamie wouldn't hear it. He had begged, cajoled, and whined until they let me stay again. Each night after that first one, Jamie had put his arm around me and told me where I was and that I was safe. He did this each and every time, and though I didn't realize it at the time, his touch had always comforted me.

"I'm sorry," I told him after a few minutes. "I just woke up a little disoriented." He scooted closer to me as we sat side by side and wrapped his arms around my shoulders, exactly as he had done when we were younger. Making a conscious effort to slow my breathing from the panicked panting, we sat awkwardly on the inflatable mattress, shivering slightly in the evening air. Jamie grabbed the top of the blanket and pulled it back over us as I gazed out into the pitch black night, feeling unnerved, vulnerable. "Before I came to live with the Schreibers, I never felt safe, ever. There was always another kid who was bigger or an adult who was meaner. Now, one of my biggest fears is that Richard and Carolyn will find out about me," I lowered my voice instinctively to a whisper, "about us, and they'll send me back." Looking up into his blue eyes, I saw my own uneasiness mirrored there.

"They wouldn't do that," he replied, but his tone was unconvincing. I nodded, acknowledging his hollow placating. Pulling me down with him so that my face was pressed into the warm hollow of his neck, Jamie lay down, and we held each other until the blissful darkness came over me once again.

"Let's unload the gear here and walk a few yards upstream," Mr. Mayfield said as he opened the trunk of their family car. "We have more of a chance catching a few there than farther downstream." He pulled out three fishing poles and an old tackle box. "Brian, why don't you grab that cooler there with the bait? Jamie, take this one with the food and such." Closing the trunk with a snap, Jamie's father led the way to a beautiful spot about twenty yards away under a giant tree. We laid the coolers back against the base, and Mr. Mayfield set the poles on the ground.

Watching Mr. Mayfield, it was hard to tell that he was related to Jamie. His receding brown hair was thin and straight while Jamie's blond, wavy hair curled and kinked in the humidity. Where Jamie was thin and wiry, Mr. Mayfield was fleshier in his khaki shorts, looking kind of like an overgrown boy scout. The only similarity between the two was that Jamie had exactly inherited his father's eyes. Mr. Mayfield's eyes, now complemented by laugh lines, were the color and shape of Jamie's. Soon we were sitting on the bank, our lines in the water, and Mr. Mayfield was telling us stories from when he and Mrs. Mayfield used to take Jamie camping when he was a kid. It was great to hear stories about Jamie from before we'd ever met.

"And then, after you and I got up to start breakfast, a raccoon got into the tent where your mama was sleeping," Mr. Mayfield choked, his laughter getting the better of him for a moment. Jamie and I were laughing too. "She screamed to high heaven and tried to run out of the tent, but she... she got caught... in the flaps. Scared you something fierce 'cause you were just a little thing, but I was cracking up as I finally got her loose. Man, she didn't talk to me for the rest of the morning for laughing at her."

"I'm going to grab a Coke from the cooler. You want anything?" Jamie asked me, still chuckling at his father's story. I told him I'd take a Coke too. "Dad?" He stood up and brushed off the backs of his shorts while I tried very hard not to notice the way his naked arms and his bare chest flexed as he did so. Quickly, I forced my eyes back to the water.

"I'll take a beer. They're kind of hidden in the bottom," Mr. Mayfield replied, his voice a little sheepish. He sounded like a kid who had been caught with his hand in the candy jar. "Just please, don't tell your mother." Jamie laughed and came back a minute later with the three cans, which he then distributed. His father sighed and opened his beer.

"You might not believe this, son, but there was a time, before you were born, that your mother would have been happy to join me in a cold one. When we were first married, we'd go out drinking and dancing with your Uncle Glenn and Aunt Peg." Jamie looked at his father with skepticism. Apparently, he couldn't believe, much like I couldn't, that Mrs. Mayfield ever drank or went dancing. The church didn't allow such things, and she was such a strong-willed woman when it came to following God's laws. Mr. Mayfield sighed, and he suddenly looked older and tired.

"When she was about seven months pregnant with you, we were coming home from your grandmother's place upstate and a deer wandered into the road ahead of us. I tried to swerve around it, but I couldn't, and we hit it head on." Even now, seventeen years later, Mr. Mayfield paled at the memory. "You and your mama almost died. It was the scariest night of my whole life. But, by the grace of God, you both came out of it alive. That night, your mama decided that Jesus spared the two of you for a reason. She's been devoted to him ever since." Jamie's father shook his head and tossed his empty beer can back toward the cooler. As an afterthought, he added, "It's not that I mind her finding religion, really; I just miss the woman I married." He looked up, realizing that he'd said that last bit out loud, maybe going a bit too far. "Jamie, son, can you grab me another beer?"

We sat quietly for a while, taking in his father's story. I was dying to talk to Jamie alone. He had almost not been born? The thought sent a sliver of ice into my stomach, chilling me through to the bone despite the heat of the afternoon. It wasn't until Jamie and I both got virtually simultaneous bites on our lines that the melancholy mood that had settled over the afternoon broke. Jamie's father jumped off of the stump that he had been using as a chair to help us reel in our catches.

All in all, we had caught about half a dozen good-sized fish. Despite my protests, Mr. Mayfield insisted I take half of them home for Richard and Carolyn. I had to say that it was a pretty good day, and I felt more comfortable with Jamie's father than I had. When I went to church with them or stayed over, it had always seemed that he and Jamie's mother were on the same page when it came to religion. It helped to know that sometimes he struggled with it too.

A few hours later, they dropped me off with a hand full of fish and a head full of questions.

"Brian, what?" Carolyn asked, a little wary, as I brought my haul into the kitchen and set the fish in the sink. To me, they didn't look like dinner; they just looked like dead fish in the sink. It was kind of gross, actually.

"Mr. Mayfield insisted that I take them. I didn't want to be rude," I told her, watching the dead eyes staring up from their stainless steel tomb.

Carolyn looked a few more times between the fish and my fairly green face and said very calmly, "So, pizza good with you for dinner?"

CHAPTER EIGHT

Nine thirty.

It was just seven minutes later than the last time I had glanced over at my clock. Reclined back on my bed with the John Marshall paperback Jamie had lent me, I tried not to think for the hundredth time that night what they were doing. Jamie was out on a date with Emma for the first time since our intimate night in the tree house. It made me physically sick to think about them together, no matter how fucking necessary it was. Honestly, more than feeling bad for myself, I felt worse for Jamie. He hadn't wanted me to know about the date at all and had been upset when his mother asked him about it in front of me earlier that day. We had been in the kitchen getting a soda from the fridge when she'd asked him what time he'd need the car.

I never said a word to him about it, even when he tried to reassure me. The pretense of dating her was hard enough without burdening him with my feelings. Before I left, however, he pulled me up to his room and pressed me against the back of the closed door. He held my face in his hands and pressed his lips to mine in long, slow, deep kisses. Never saying a word, he just did everything he could to make me feel his love, to make me feel how special I was to him. It really helped to quell the hot molten jealousy that burned through my veins.

That was, until I was alone with nothing to dam the flood of my own imagination.

As the numbers on my clock had changed, marking the passage of each and every minute they spent together, I tortured myself by living their date in my mind. At seven, I imagined him at her house, making small talk with her father while he waited for her to finish getting ready. Of course, when she came into the room, he would kiss her on the cheek and tell her how pretty her mousy hair looked. He would hold the door for her as they left, assuring her father that he would be a gentleman and have her home on time. I'd love to just slam the door in her face and take him on our own date.

At seven thirty, I thought about them having dinner together at some secluded, dimly lit restaurant where he would hold her hand as they decided between the pasta and the chicken. Of course Jamie and I would have been taken out and beaten for that same handholding. The injustice of it rankled me, and I looked around my room for something to distract me from the mounting anger.

The book managed to hold my attention for about an hour, at which time I imagined they'd be at the movies. Emma would probably pick something sickeningly romantic, or maybe something scary so that Jamie would have to hold and console her. *While he sat in the theater with his arms around her, trying to calm her fears, would she turn her face and kiss him?* Maybe they were making out in the back row, while I sat gripping his paperback tight enough to rip the spine.

When I glanced at the clock again, it was nearly ten. Surely the movie was over. *What would they be doing?* Jamie didn't have to have Emma home until eleven since school was out. I tried desperately not to imagine them driving out to the bluffs. *The kissing I had learned to tolerate, but what if she talked him into something more?* I could just see her wondering if maybe he didn't like girls because he didn't want to feel her up. Nausea made my stomach churn at the thought of her hands under his shirt on his perfect bare chest or of her unzipping his jeans.

Jamie would do anything to protect us, to protect me.

Damn it, it was supposed to be me he was out with, not her. Not her!

I doubted that I would ever really know what happened between them because Jamie would do everything he could to spare my feelings. There was no way I would be able to sleep that night with my mind racing with all of the possible things that... girl had done with my Jamie. Setting my useless paperback book aside, I went down the hall to the bathroom and pulled the allergy medication that Carolyn used from the medicine cabinet. I'd seen her take it enough times to know that it was supposed to make you sleepy. I popped two pills from the foil wrapping and took them with a paper cup of water before returning to my room. I'd never taken anything like that before, but I just couldn't fucking stand the pictures in my head anymore.

Lying down on my bed, I closed my eyes and dreamed of my own date with Jamie.

"Let's go out," I suggested quietly to Jamie as we finished the supper dishes. Tonight was the first time we'd seen each other in a week. He had been spending time with Emma, building the farce and adding to the charade. Their displays of affection continued to irk me, but I kept my feelings to myself; Jamie didn't need the added stress of my discontent. The imaginary relationship, imaginary to him at least, was taking its toll. He felt deep-seated guilt for lying to her; I could hear it as he slept during our nights together. Tossing and turning, moaning and murmuring in his sleep, it was fairly obvious that his conscience, his soul, was tormented. I didn't feel the need to add to the torment by asking if he'd felt her up yet, so mostly we avoided talking about her. Deep down, I didn't really want to know anyway.

"What do you mean?" he asked, setting the plate he had been washing back into the hot soapy water before turning to look at me. It took me a moment to stop imagining those warm suds over his naked hip and stomach. My mind wandered briefly, as it had done so often of late, over what it would be like when we didn't have to hide anymore. Heaven could be defined simply by taking a long shower with Jamie and not having to worry about parents or anyone else coming between us. His expectant expression caught my eye.

"On a date," I explained in a low voice so that Richard and Carolyn wouldn't hear me. "I want to go out, just you and me, maybe dinner and a movie?" I had been thinking about asking him for weeks without any real expectations, but now that it was out there, my hope grew exponentially. I had been saving the pocket money I'd received from Carolyn for weeks now in order to pay for it. Since I was asking him, I would be the one paying. He would still have to drive, but it would be a real date, just us.

"Are you fucking crazy?" he growled at me under his breath. "Why don't we just go ahead and bring along the bats they can use to beat us to death with?" His tone was cold, mocking. I was instantly disappointed, and angry.

I had no answer for him.

I turned, drying the glass in my hand, so he wouldn't see the pain in my face. This was just one more thing that girl could have with Jamie that I could not. They could get married, have kids, and still be invited to the Sunday barbecue. Jamie and I could have none of that; we would always be outcast because of what we felt for each other. We couldn't even have one simple fucking date. Everything was about her, not about us.

According to the clock on the microwave, we continued to do the dishes, not speaking, for exactly seventeen minutes. Focusing on the clock instead of Jamie's silence and anger made the time actually pass instead of solidify like the feeling in my chest. I hung the damp towel on one of the drawer handles while he rinsed out the sink.

Then I just stood there, waiting.

"Let's take the garbage out," he mumbled, pulling the half-empty bag out the back door, which he left open behind him. I followed reluctantly, feeling once again like a petulant child. I fucking hated feeling like that, hated that we were forced to resort to talking about our love life over the garbage cans in our back alley.

"We shouldn't have to hide," I told him once he'd pushed the bag down into the can and replaced the lid. He sighed, and despite the fact that he was only seventeen years old, he sounded weary.

"I agree, we shouldn't. In a perfect world, it should be you that I'm holding hands with while walking down the street. It would be you that I'm kissing after a romantic date. We don't live in a perfect world, Brian. In this world, in the reality that we live in, if anyone realizes just how much I care for you, it could mean both of our lives. Is one date, one night spent in the company of others, really worth that?"

"I'm not talking about sitting in your fucking lap in the movie theater! I'm talking about going out for crappy fast food and an action flick that no self-respecting girl would go see with us. I'm talking about just maybe getting a little bit of what that girl gets with you. Apparently, that's all we deserve, and I won't fucking touch you." For the first time, rather than looking down and getting teary, I looked him straight in the eye.

"Brian, I—" he started, but I cut him off.

"Let's go inside. Maybe we can sit at opposite sides of the couch and watch a movie." I held my arm out, palm up, indicating for him to go first. He looked at me and then began walking back up the weed-strewn sidewalk to the house. His footsteps were slow and heavy as we made our way up the back porch, but instead of going inside, I leaned in and closed the heavy wooden door and sat down on the worn wicker couch.

Jamie sat next to me and, under the cover of the dark night, reached over and held my hand. We sat looking out at the backyard and listening to the crickets for a long time. Then he squeezed my hand, and when I looked over at him, his face was impassive.

"I'll pick you up Friday night at seven, Brian."

I nodded. I wanted to say more, but he squeezed my hand lightly again and then got up and walked into the house. I sat outside a few minutes longer, knowing that when I went back into the house, he would be gone home.

He was.

The next two days went painfully slowly without him. He was upset, that much was certain, but more than that, he was scared. He was also right. If anyone suspected that we were more than just friends, they would hurt us. It was a whole new level of selfish for me. Not only was I putting myself at risk, but Jamie as well, and for what? We were perfectly happy in our tree house. I just wanted that one small thing, one small victory against them, those that hated us without knowing it. Emma Mosely had something of Jamie that I couldn't have, and it pissed me off because I wanted that kind of acknowledgement from him. I just hoped, no, prayed, that it wouldn't end up costing either of us more than we could afford to give.

By ten past seven on Friday night, I was starting to worry about Jamie. He had been late for school a few times and had come right down to the wire getting ready for church, but I felt unnerved that he wasn't here yet. This date was important, to me, to us, and he knew that. He would have made an effort to be on time, wouldn't he? The thought that someone had found out about us, that someone had hurt him, sent a chill through me. Stopping myself for what must have been the tenth time, I didn't call him. I couldn't appear too eager just to go out for burgers and an action movie. His parents might wonder. My emotions were going to be our undoing; I would just have to wait.

Five minutes later the soft knock on the door left me with residual anger and a lot of relief. The fear had burned off into anger, mostly at myself for being so ridiculous. The relief swelled as I opened the door and saw his perfect features. He was smiling, almost ruefully, as he stood there in a perfectly fitting T-shirt, one that I had not seen before, matched with jeans and canvas tennis shoes. With the way he was dressed, you wouldn't think he was going on a date, but I saw the differences. He had made an effort to tame his shaggy blond hair. Similar care had been taken about my own appearance. For the first time since he'd said he'd pick me up, I felt hope.

"Bye, Carolyn!" I called over my shoulder in the general direction of the kitchen. I heard a noncommittal response as Jamie led me out of the house. He didn't touch me, or even look at me, as we walked down the steps to the walkway. While I knew it was just for the benefit of the neighbors, I wondered if maybe I had made a mistake in asking him to go out on a date. I nearly ran into him as he took a sharp right and headed toward the back of the house, and I noticed for the first time that his car wasn't out front.

"Are we walking?" I asked cautiously. "It's going to take us all night to get to the theater that way." Making a joke out of it would help take away the sting. Maybe his parents wouldn't give him the car, or maybe he had changed his mind. When we walked around the corner of the house, he led me back up the driveway, where I saw the car sitting under the canopy of elm trees that stood sentinel near the old garage. Surprised, I walked to the passenger side of the car while he got in the driver's side. I waited for him to tell me why he'd chosen this location in which to park. Usually, he just parked on the street, never in the drive.

"I'm sorry that I was late," Jamie said as he reached behind my seat. He was so close as he searched the floorboard that I couldn't stop myself from placing a small kiss on his neck. Thankfully we were surrounded by trees on one side and the house on the other. I couldn't believe my boldness; all it would take would be Carolyn looking out the kitchen window, and it would be all over. Chastising myself, I sat back in the seat and looked nervously up toward the house and saw nothing.

Then the rose in Jamie's hand passed in front of my eyes.

"It took me forever to get this out of my mother's garden without anyone seeing me." He set the rose on my leg under the line of sight provided by the car windows. I didn't know what to say; I was relieved that he was no longer angry. Setting the rose on the dash, I reached over to hold his hand because it was the one thing we could do inconspicuously. But instead, he took his keys and started the car, his face impassive as he backed out of the drive. For the rest of the ride to dinner, I stared out the window, feeling dejected. I know I had no right, I had practically forced the whole situation on him, but I had been planning this night, anticipating this time with him for weeks. It felt like everything had gone wrong before we ever even got out of the driveway.

When we pulled into the parking lot at the fast food place he'd decided on, I was disappointed to see that it was almost full. We would have to be on our best behavior. He got out of the car and started to walk toward the door. Quickly I got out and followed him, feeling a lot like a stray puppy trying to get some kind of attention.

The place was packed with people, mostly teenagers that I recognized from school but none I knew particularly well. They didn't give us a second glance as we stood near the counter. Since I was the one paying and the place was almost overflowing, Jamie gave me his order and then went to find a booth. He walked off with his shoulders hunched and head down. I hated it. He was scared, and it was my fault.

I thought that I would feel shy or awkward around him. First dates were supposed to be about getting to know each other, but we already knew everything about each other, especially because we had already been intimate. *What was left to talk about, to discover about each other?*

I set the tray down in front of Jamie, and he glanced around nervously, and I felt a tightening in my chest. Sitting across from him, I took our food from the tray and then set it near the back of the table. Jamie didn't say anything as he stared at the paper-wrapped burger.

"Do you want to go home?" I whispered across the cheap Formica table. Raising his head, he looked at me, and I expected him to admonish me, to tell me that this was my fucking idea in the first place, but he just shook his head and opened his food. I glanced around to make sure no one was looking our way, and then I picked up my chicken sandwich. As I took the first bite, I slid my feet forward so that they were entwined with his. On such a busy night with so many customers, no one would notice how close our feet were under the table. After what felt like an eternity, his foot moved, caressing mine. Still not looking up, he turned up his mouth in a small smile, and I relaxed against the seat.

"What time does the movie start?" I asked, trying to strike up some kind of conversation. He hadn't spoken to me since giving me his mumbled order. It didn't matter what we talked about, I just wanted to hear his voice. The fear that I had pushed Jamie too far insisting we go out, the fear that someone might see us there, was threatening to drown me. There was also the ever-present fear that I would fall even harder for him, and that when he did leave me for whatever reason, it would be that much harder to bear.

"It starts at 8:15. We should have plenty of time," he said between sips of his soda. Not being able to think of anything else to say, I nodded.

"Did you see that Boltz is coming out soon?" he asked, trying to keep the conversation going. He knew full well that I wasn't really into video games, but I was glad that he was making the effort. The tension in his shoulders had dissipated slightly, but he still looked wary. I rubbed my foot against his under the table, trying to show how much I appreciated him being here with me.

"No, I didn't know that," I told him, and he smiled, rubbing my leg again with his shoe. I relaxed somewhat at his touch, and that broke down the invisible barrier that had been between us.

We talked about everything and nothing for the next twenty minutes while we ate. Occasionally someone stopped by the table to say hi, and Jamie would tense, but generally we were left alone. The movie would be worse. Being in a dark theater alone with him and not being able to touch him would almost be physical torture. Too bad we hadn't decided to go and play paintball instead. I'm sure he would probably have loved to shoot me right then.

On the long drive to the theater, we held hands, reveling in the physical contact, an indulgence we were rarely afforded. The perfect way his hand fit into mine helped to ease the dull ache of fear pressing on my chest. It was Friday night, and the theater parking lot was more crowded than the restaurant had been. I sighed, and Jamie squeezed my hand once before letting go. All of a sudden, I didn't want to go inside. As I reached for the door handle, the fear surrounded me like a physical presence, pressing against me and escalating to the point of panic. The tightness in my chest made it hard to breathe. Jamie noticed that I hadn't gotten out of the car and came around to my door, opening it. I still couldn't get out. *Someone was going to know; they'd be able to tell, and then they would hurt Jamie, and it would be my fault.*

Why the hell hadn't I just left well enough alone?

"We have to go in if we want to get good seats," Jamie said quietly as he leaned on the top of the open door, an old black sweatshirt in his hand.

"I don't care about good seats. You were right, maybe we should just go home," I said, voicing my concern. We'd pushed our luck far enough.

"No. You were right, we shouldn't have to hide. I'm just as scared, Brian. It would kill me if someone hurt you because of me. We can sit in the balcony, away from the others, and we should be okay." His words came out in a breathless rush, and before I knew it, he was tugging my T-shirt to get me out of the car. I was sure he would have taken my hand if there hadn't been so many people around, because it strayed toward me several times before we reached the front doors.

Resigned, I followed Jamie past the rows and rows of cars on the way to the door of the theater, relaxing a bit when I didn't see anyone I knew. We split up once we were through the doors; I bought our tickets while Jamie went to the concession stand. It didn't matter that we'd just eaten dinner; popcorn and soda were a rite of passage for moviegoers everywhere. Since we weren't able to go out often, we were damn sure going to make the very best of it.

When I got through the line and back to where Jamie was waiting, I handed him his ticket, and he handed me my popcorn and soda. Opting for the balcony, we climbed the long, decrepit stairway until we reached the back of the sloping balcony.

It was deserted.

We took the stairs down the side of the rows of seats, past discarded popcorn buckets and sticky stains of spilled beverages, to the very front row. Propping our feet up on the railing, we sat in two seats directly in the middle of the row. Every few minutes we glanced back over our shoulders, but no one else entered the balcony. We looked down over the railing and saw that the main theater area was also pretty empty.

This movie must really suck, and I, for one, was grateful.

We settled back in the seats as the lights went down, working on the popcorn that we were forbidden to share. Within the first ten minutes of the movie, we knew where it was going, a melding of heterosexual machismo and sex, but I didn't care. I was on a date with Jamie. No matter how bad the movie was, it was perfect because I was there with him.

Just as the ninjas, or whatever they were, back-flipped onto the screen for the third time, Jamie pulled out the generic, black-hooded sweatshirt that he had brought in. At first, I didn't realize why he'd bothered. The theater was air conditioned but still not cold enough for a sweatshirt. I was even more confused when he laid it over his legs rather than putting it on. Then as he straightened it out, he took my hand underneath it, and I understood. He wanted us to be able to hold hands during the movie without taking the chance of anyone seeing the small gesture of affection.

It thrilled me that he was holding my hand in this place, around people, even if there were only a few and they weren't in the balcony. The date meant as much to him as it did to me, but it saddened me as well. *Why did being together, here in this second-run theater, or anywhere else, have to constitute such a risk for us?* What I wanted more than anything was to lean over and rest my head on his shoulder while we finished watching the movie, but that would be like a neon sign flashing "fag" over our heads. I had to be content to take what I could get.

So I was.

Sitting in the theater, we held hands under the cover of the sweatshirt and ate popcorn for the next hour. Even though the movie was awful, it was the best time I'd had in a long time. For that short period, we felt somewhat normal, like our feelings for each other weren't some kind of abomination, but rather something beautiful.

We continued to hold hands on the drive back to my house. However, in the safety of the car, we didn't need the camouflage of the sweatshirt. Every once in a while, on a deserted stretch of road where no one could see, he would bring our entwined hands up to his lips or to caress my cheek. My heart swelled with each gesture. Just before reaching the Crayford city limits, he glanced around and pulled to the side of the road.

"I can't kiss you goodnight on your doorstep like you deserve," he said quietly, letting go of my hand for the first time since we left the theater. "It will have to be here."

Jamie cupped both sides of my face in his hands, rubbing my cheek with his thumbs. Watching my face for a long minute before he leaned in, he captured my lips with his own, and every feeling of love and sexual desire escalated into a slow burn of heat through my skin. God, I loved the way he kissed me, like nothing else in the world mattered. The smell of popcorn still clung to his clothes, but there was something else, body wash or shampoo, something uniquely Jamie. The passion in our kiss continued to spiral as our tongues explored, danced against the other's, and everything else was blocked out by its all-encompassing heat. Sun, moon, and stars took a backseat to him. Sacrificing my lunches for weeks was definitely worth it, even if just to have this kiss at the end of our very first date.

Jamie stopped the kiss before either of us got too carried away. Even though it was more chaste than I would have preferred, I got what I needed: his love, his comfort, and my very first real date with the boy who I could not live without.

The next morning, I was still thinking about my date with Jamie, holding his hand at the theater and kissing him in the car. I had just decided to jump in the shower and think about it more thoroughly when I was interrupted by a knock on my bedroom door.

"Brian, could I talk to you for a minute?" Richard asked as he stood in the doorway. Immediately, I was uneasy; my foster father rarely wanted to have a heart-to-heart, covering mostly superficial things at dinner but never anything that really mattered. Those talks were left up to Carolyn. It meant that he wanted to talk to me about something that Carolyn didn't feel comfortable discussing with me... like sex.

Oh God, he knew about Jamie.

"Sure, Richard," I said, trying not to let my voice crack from the fear that was now coursing through me.

Please don't send me away. Please don't tear me away from Jamie.

He was the first person in my life to ever truly love me, and I wasn't going to give that up without a fight. I would be seventeen in just over two weeks, we could tough it out one more year, or I could run away from Richard and Carolyn and hide. It was as simple as that. Richard turned and motioned for me to follow him. The sinking feeling deepened when I saw that we were headed for his office, even more so when we headed to his computer. He sat down in his desk chair.

"A few days ago, I wanted to do some research on a rare gastrointestinal condition that I was trying to treat at the hospital. When I started to type in the search criteria, look what starts to auto-populate." He typed in "g" and then "a" and to my horror "gay men" showed up as one of the recent searches. My palms started to sweat as he showed me the browser's history, including some photos I was sure he never wanted to see.

I stood there, stunned.

The shame washed through me, and my face reddened. My eyes filled with tears. Trying not to cry, I looked out of the nearby window onto the street below as my mind went numb.

"Was this you?" he asked quietly, and there was absolutely no point in denying it. It's not like Carolyn was going to come up here and search for "gay men." I nodded, feeling the first of the tears fall. I knew from years of experience that it only took one phone call for them to get rid of me, and I would never see Jamie again. Belatedly, it occurred to me to tell him that I had done the search for a school report, but he would not have believed me. No teacher in his right mind would assign it, and the guilt was already etched onto my face that was streaked liberally with tears. I hung my head, waiting for it.

"Then there are a few things that I'd like to talk to you about." I nodded, completely unable to look at him. He was going to send me back to the state, return me like a defective toaster. *Well, why the fuck not? I was a throwaway kid, right? Why, when I was finally happy, when I finally had someone who loved me?* All I could think about was Jamie. *Would they even tell him why they had sent me away?* Tracing a line in the worn carpeting with the front of my shoe, I heard my blood pounding in my ears. Desperately I wished Jamie was there with me, but of course, I also didn't because he would be in trouble then too. Obviously there was nothing about Jamie in those searches, but it seemed like a simple leap to me, like there was a sign on my forehead.

"Are you using condoms?" Richard asked, breaking into my thoughts. My head jerked up, and I stared at him. It took me several seconds to even compose anything near a coherent reply.

"I don't... I mean I haven't... I've never...." I spluttered, entirely unable to convey to him that I had never had sex.

"Brian, I don't want you to think that I'm prying into your sex life. I just want to make sure that you're being safe. There are so many things that could happen if you're not careful, not the least of which are HIV and AIDS. You're a good kid, and I really care about you; I want to make sure you're going to be okay." It was the longest conversation that

I think we'd ever had on any subject other than sports. To me, it was the most important conversation we'd ever had. He didn't hate me; he was trying to look out for me. For the first time since I'd come to live with him, he was being a father to me. I couldn't even come close to expressing the gratitude I felt for him, but I was sure as hell going to try.

Once I had decided to be honest, the dam broke, and everything that I had been holding inside for the last six months came spilling out. At first, my confession was just a small stream, breaching the cracks in my resolve, but as my words gained momentum, it turned into a flood. It felt so fucking good just to talk about it. So, I told him about my feelings for Jamie and about Pastor Moore's sermon. I told him about being terrified all the time that someone would find out, that Jamie's parents would find out. I told him about the girl at school that Jamie was pretending to date. However, I didn't tell him what Jamie and I had done together sexually. That was something private, sacred, between Jamie and me.

We talked for more than an hour, and I learned more about him in that time than I had since he'd picked me up at the state home almost six years before. He hadn't grown up in Alabama; originally, he was from New York and had come to Alabama to go to college. While at college, he'd met Carolyn and decided that he wanted to stay in the South and build a life with her.

"See, when I was a boy, my parents had my life all planned out for me," Richard said, his eyes far away. "But I wasn't meant to lead the life that they'd planned. They were both in law, and my father wanted to see my name on the door right below his. To say that I disappointed them by going into medicine would be an understatement. They found my choice to remain here in Alabama to practice a calamity. What destroyed my relationship with them, however, was their attitude toward Carolyn. I believe that people should live their lives on their own terms, Brian. Whether those terms are heterosexual, homosexual, law, medicine, etcetera, the choice is up to you."

More than half of our conversation was centered on the mechanics of sex, gay sex in particular. As a doctor, he had a unique perspective on the subject. Using a banana, he taught me the right way to put on a condom, leaving space at the end for the semen. We discussed different kinds of lubricants, condoms, and some of the more sensitive topics of sex, so I could make good choices and be safe. I felt completely awkward asking him questions, but he answered every one with a clinical detachment. It was easier for him to talk about it in the abstract, because I knew talking about it with Jamie and I in mind was uncomfortable for him.

"Are you going to tell Carolyn?" I asked once we were finished with the awkward topics. Richard, with his gay New York friend, might understand about my sexual orientation, but Carolyn was a good, pure, Southern woman. *What would she think of me if she knew that Jamie and I were in an intimate relationship? Would she be appalled? Disgusted? Scared of what her sewing circle were going to think?*

"No, you should tell her," he said, standing up from his desk chair and heading for the door. "You'll find her more sympathetic than you might imagine. She was brought up with strict Southern values, but she also has a mind of her own and strong opinions about certain topics. But she believes, like I do, that you should live life on your own terms. When she gave up her dream of being a child psychologist to marry me and raise our son, she weighed the choice carefully and did what her heart told her to do. When our son died, she questioned every decision she made. She just wasn't the same woman."

Richard's eyes were sad as he spoke of the death of his son and what it had done to the woman that he obviously loved more than anything. "One day, she was working in her garden in the backyard, and a little girl wandered into our driveway. We had never seen the girl before, and she appeared to be lost and unkempt. Carolyn asked the little girl where she lived, but the girl wouldn't speak. Finally, we got the police involved and found out that this poor lost child had been abandoned by her mother the day before. It was then that Carolyn knew that she wanted to help the girl, and we applied to be her foster parents." He smiled at the memory. "So, having been through more than most people should in one lifetime, Carolyn has a different perspective on life than most people in this little town."

"Thank you, Richard," I told him earnestly. In spite of his discomfort, he had helped to calm some of my fears and answer all of my questions. I couldn't have asked for a better counselor.

I stayed in the office for a while, watching the sun set through the open curtains, thinking about our discussion. *What kinds of implications would it have for Jamie and me?* I had just told our secret to an outside person. The more people who know a secret, the less secure the secret. We only had one more year, and then we could be together; we had to hold on. Of course we would still have to worry about hatred and bigotry, but we would be in charge of our own destinies and lives together.

I stalled for weeks, wondering how Carolyn would take my revelation. I was most afraid of disappointing her. She had always worked so hard to try and make me a good person, to make up for the life that I had been given, and I was about to tell her that I was flawed, in more ways than she'd originally thought. Not only was I concerned about disappointing her, but I questioned whether or not I should tell her about my relationship with Jamie. *That wasn't my thing to tell, but what if she asked, or what if she guessed? Would she look at him differently once she knew?*

Even though I wasn't staying over at Jamie's every weekend, I was still spending an increasing amount of time with him. It was summer; we didn't have anything to do, so we spent almost all of our time together. Hanging out at the Schreibers', or sometimes at Jamie's, always making sure we weren't too obvious. We tried to avoid the tree house as much as possible because we didn't want to give any indication about what was going on in it when I stayed the night. Our sexual exploits were getting more and more adventurous. We hadn't gone all the way yet, but we had gotten each other off in a variety of ways during the times I had stayed over. The last time, we had pleased each other with our mouths at the same time. It was so fucking hot, and I had tried my best to stay focused on pleasing him, but I kept losing my concentration because of what he was doing to me. Just thinking about it made me excited.

The biggest problem we had right then was Emma, as she was tired of Jamie avoiding her to spend time with me. She had also asked about why I had run from the band room that last day before school ended. It didn't take a rocket scientist to know I had been upset when I'd seen them kissing. Emma was a bright girl, and without some kind of explanation, she would begin to draw her own conclusions. Jamie had dismissed it, explaining that I had been embarrassed and wanted to get out of the room, and that I hadn't been feeling well, telling her that the next day we discovered I had the stomach flu. Emma accepted his explanation because Jamie had an honest face and rarely lied. Well, before we had started dating he had rarely lied, but it had become a knee-jerk response. I hated that I had done that to him.

I had made him dishonest.

Then Jamie had told her that I may have a crush on her friend Brenda Sears. Brenda was a shy, rather frumpy girl who Emma seemed to have a soft spot for. His ingenious bit of fantasy had derailed Emma from figuring out my feelings for Jamie. So, once again, Jamie and I had a double date for Saturday night. To me, the only good thing about it was that Jamie and I would be able to spend the night alone afterwards.

Between sweet and almost chaste kisses in the small confines of my upstairs bedroom, among the pieces of the new model we were working on, he reminded me that we had to go out with them in order to be together. We had to pretend we were just like everyone else, and at seventeen, that mold that we were forcing ourselves into included dating teenage girls. I consoled myself that at the very least, she was a nice girl and not Karen Simmons. He sat beside me on the edge of my bed, and I rested my head on his shoulder, completely lost in the scent of his soap, and reminded myself that it was just one more year.

My seventeenth birthday was one week away, and then just one more year and no one could tell me who I could and couldn't be with. I would be my own man.

Well, really, I would be Jamie's man.

"There's always the church fair; we could take them there," I suggested to Jamie. I sat back against his chest in the tree house. We'd decided to take the chance and sneak up to our sanctuary for a little alone time before getting ready to take Emma and Brenda out on our double date. While I was following the conversation, my attention was more focused on the way his hard chest felt behind my back and the way his arms felt around me. It was warm but not uncomfortable with the fan blowing.

"You sure you want to be around the holy masses?" he asked, kissing me lightly behind the ear. I turned my head and caught his lips in a slow, deep kiss before he could sit back against the wall. He smiled down at me, filling me with a warmth that had nothing to do with the hot summer day.

"I think that would be less awkward than going to the movies. What if Emma decides that we should split up once we get there so she can have her way with you in the dark?" I was only half serious, but it still caused a little bile to rise up in my throat. I couldn't imagine the thought of sitting in a dark theater with some girl I didn't want to be with while the guy I did want to be with was making out with someone else.

"I wouldn't let that happen, but I see your point. Being outside around other people may give both of them less expectations." He pressed his lips against my neck and just held me back against him. I put my hands up on his arms, holding them there, wishing that we never had to leave our tree house, but that just wasn't how life worked.

"It's six o'clock, and I need to shower before we pick up the girls at seven," Jamie said, still nuzzling my neck, holding me tighter as if he'd read my mind about never wanting to leave.

"Okay," I replied, reluctantly attempting to slide forward out of his arms and get up off the inflatable mattress. Jamie held fast, not letting me move.

"Yeah, ten more minutes," he said in almost a growl as he pulled me to the side with him, laying us both down on the mattress. I laughed and rolled onto my back so that he hovered over me. Leaning down, Jamie tilted his head slightly to the right and came closer. He stopped just short of a kiss, his mouth slightly open and his lips turned up in a smirk as I strained up to kiss him. Moaning, he pushed me back and kissed me slowly.

"Tonight I want you to remember this moment whenever you feel like she has something you don't. I want you to remember that deep in my heart, I'm wishing that it was you and only you," Jamie whispered as his lips molded against mine, licking, teasing, tasting with a gentle sensuality that made my breath catch in my throat. First, he caught my upper lip between his, sucking lightly before doing the same with my lower lip. His thumb stroked my cheek as his hand curved around the side of my face, and I gave everything to him. My love, my affection, my very soul was his.

It was actually more like twenty minutes before I climbed down the tree house ladder in a bit of a daze. My lips were swollen and my hair was a mess, but I was happy as I jogged home to get cleaned up. Jamie and I might have to have two giggling and annoying girls between us at that fair tonight for the sake of propriety, but at least we would be together. It was infinitely better than staying home and wondering what the fuck was happening with my boyfriend and that girl.

My boyfriend.

The word was so inadequate but at the same time so exciting to me. Jamie was my boyfriend, and I was prepared to do anything I had to in order to keep that, including taking Suzie fucking Sunshine to the fair.

"I think that's a great idea," Emma said as she pulled Brenda through the front door of Brenda's small house and onto the porch. Brenda looked nothing short of terrified as she stood behind Emma.

"Brenda, you make sure you're in this house by ten thirty. Don't make me come looking for you!" a woman's voice bellowed from inside the house, and Brenda tried to make herself even smaller. She stood huddled against the closed screen door, her long black hair shielding her from Jamie and me as we waited on the steps. Emma looked back through the closed door while pulling Brenda toward us.

"Let's go," she said quietly, and we stood aside in order to let them pass, a look of resignation passing between Jamie and me behind their backs as the four of us made our way to the Ford. Brenda climbed into the back with me, and we looked at each other shyly before looking away again. The whole situation just felt awkward as I watched Emma reaching over to straighten Jamie's collar, her fingers lingering on his neck. Closing my eyes for just a second, I remembered what Jamie had told me and thought about our sweet and loving kiss earlier that afternoon. The jealousy was slowly replaced with the warmth that I always associated with Jamie's love.

I stayed lost in that feeling all the way to the church.

We pulled into the soccer field across the street from the fair where Emma's and Jamie's fathers were waving cars in to park. Mr. Mayfield waved to us when we passed and pulled into the next available makeshift spot. Brenda and Emma waited for Jamie and me to walk around to the other side of the car and open their doors. I held my hand out, and Brenda took it but dropped it the moment she was out of the car, whispering a thank you as she went back to stand next to Emma.

Emma was whispering, probably some kind of encouragement, to Brenda as they wound their way through the maze of parked cars headed toward the brightly lit tents ahead. Jamie and I followed, letting the girls decide where they wanted to go first. The closer side of the fair held all of the games, including a bingo tent, pull tab booth, and some ring tosses where you could win a goldfish. In the center were food booths with all kinds of sodas, hot dogs, pretzels, and funnel cakes. The games slowly gave way to rides for the rest of the carnival. The initial rides were all for smaller kids, but we could hear the screaming from the bigger rides. Huge mechanical boats and cages swung high in the air at the end of the strip, making me very glad I hadn't eaten before leaving the house.

"Okay, girls, where to first?" Jamie asked with a heart-stopping smile. Instead of looking at him, I focused my attention on Brenda. After all, *she* was my date, not Jamie. Brenda continued to look at her shoes, and I fought the desire to roll my eyes. Emma came to her rescue by saying that we should win them something at the games.

The awkwardness lasted for the next hour while we walked around exploring the different booths and talking to friends who were also walking around the fair. When we got to the big rides at the end, we had to split up to get onto the Ferris wheel, so we let Jamie and Emma get on first. As the ride operator lowered the bar onto their laps, I noticed that Brenda visibly relaxed a little. Her shoulders lost some of their tension, and she let out a long breath. I looked down at her, and to my surprise, she smiled.

"He... uhmmm... Jamie makes me nervous." I just stared at her. Jamie was one of the sweetest guys at school. Laidback and funny, he would never be intentionally mean to anyone. Everyone liked him.

"Why would Jamie make you nervous?" I asked, trying not to make the question sound harsh, merely curious. She obviously didn't know anything about Jamie. Besides, I was the one she was supposed to be nervous about, wasn't I?

"I don't know; he's so good-looking and confident. He's like a celebrity at school; everyone knows him. What if...." She trailed off as the ride came to a stop and it was our turn to get on. I followed her up the rickety metal stairs to where the operator was holding open the gate. Giving him our tickets, we stepped through and sat down in the car. The operator dropped the bar over us and locked it, not giving us another glance as he grabbed the lever and started the ride

As we floated backwards and up the rear of the massive wheel, I turned a little in my seat to look at Brenda. She was looking out over the fair with a soft smile.

"What if, what?" I asked her quietly.

"I'm sorry?" she said, more question than statement.

"You said that Jamie is like a celebrity at school, and then 'what if'. What if, what?" I asked again.

"What if... what if he doesn't like me? I don't really have any friends as it is," she replied, still looking out over the fair as we slowly reached the top of the wheel.

"Jamie isn't like that." I wanted to reassure her, because I knew exactly what it was like not to have many friends, to have people avoid you because they thought you weren't good enough. "There isn't a mean-spirited bone in him." She finally took her eyes off of the lights of the fair to look at me.

"You guys are pretty close, aren't you?" I hesitated a little before I answered, knowing that she was only talking about being close friends but wanting to phrase my answer carefully.

"Jamie and I have been best friends since we were eleven. We do pretty much everything together," I told her, making sure that I stuck to the truth because I didn't lie well.

"It must be really nice to be close to someone like that," she said wistfully. "My mom and I just moved here last year, and I haven't really gotten close to anyone. I hate being alone all the time." She clapped a hand over her mouth and looked a little embarrassed. "Oh, God, I'm sorry." Sitting back in the seat, I was surprised when she started to laugh.

"What's so funny?" I asked, smiling at her in my confusion.

"This is one heck of a first date. First, I don't talk for an hour, and then I whine about not being popular," she said and then snorted out a giggle. I started to laugh; I couldn't help it. *God, if she only knew the half of it.* Reaching over to hold her hand, I decided that I liked Brenda. Even if we could never be anything more, she could be a good friend.

"I know what that's like. Everyone knows that the Schreibers are my foster parents, so I'm just the kid they got saddled with. The only reason anyone talks to me is because of Jamie," I told her with a shrug. We talked for a few more turns of the wheel about life at school as an outcast and found that we had quite a lot in common.

"I know what you mean," I told her when she mentioned sitting alone in the lunch room. "The few times that Jamie is out sick during the year, I sit by myself. He's really my only friend."

"Not the only one," she said quietly. "I'd like to be your friend, if you'll let me." The Ferris wheel was starting to slow as it reached the top again, and Brenda scooted closer to me on the seat. I looked into her face, which, when it wasn't covered by her hair, was kind of nice. She wanted me to kiss her, I could tell from the way she leaned in, the way she looked at my lips. Feeling a little sick at the thought of kissing someone other than Jamie, I decided that there was no point putting off the inevitable. Working up my nerve, I took a deep breath. Just as the wheel began to move again and Brenda's face fell in disappointment, I leaned forward and pressed my lips to hers.

It was so different than kissing Jamie; she was soft and delicate. Not sure what to do with my hands, I put one on her face as I would with Jamie, and I stroked her cheek with my fingers. She sighed a little and kissed me harder. The kiss didn't turn me on, like it did when Jamie kissed me, but it was nice, comforting, in a way. We pulled away when the ride came to a stop again, and I smiled at her. She beamed at me, and then the operator opened the bar across our laps and I looked up. I saw Emma, practically bouncing as she stood next to a shocked-looking Jamie. He was pale and drawn, and even with the carefully strewn lights around him, I could tell that there were tears in his eyes.

For the briefest second I wanted to feel vindication, because seeing me kiss that girl, he knew how I felt when he was out with Emma, but I couldn't. All I could feel was sadness. He looked heartbroken and even a little sick. In the time it took for Brenda and me to walk down the stairs and reach them, he had schooled his features into a mask. I could see the pain in his eyes, but on the outside he looked happy and ready for more fun.

I wasn't sure how much more fun I could stand.

Finally, thankfully, the evening wound down after a last walk through the food stands for elephant ears. The girls didn't seem to notice that Jamie and I only picked at ours before throwing them in a nearby overflowing trash can. We held their hands as we made our way back to the car, Emma nearly beside herself to see Brenda holding my hand. When we reached Brenda's house, where Emma would be staying the night, I walked Brenda up to the door while Jamie stayed in the car to kiss Emma goodnight. I kissed Brenda lightly on the lips and told her I'd had a nice time. She said that she'd had a nice time as well and wondered if we could do it again sometime, maybe without Jamie and Emma. I gave her a noncommittal shrug, my stomach in knots about having to do it all over again.

Emma was practically skipping as she passed me on the sidewalk and said, "Night, Bri."

Jamie was quiet as he drove us back to his house. Of course, I was always glad for the opportunity to stay the night with him, but tonight I knew it was particularly important. Jamie was upset, and I couldn't imagine going home and lying in my bed, staring at the cracks in my ceiling, just thinking about him. I wanted to be with him so that I could hold him and we could talk about it.

He shut off the ignition and, without waiting for me to follow, walked to the tree house and climbed the ladder. I followed quickly, and when I closed the trapdoor behind me, Jamie was already taking off his clothes and throwing them angrily across the room. When only his boxers remained, he crawled onto the mattress, facing the wall, and pulled up the sheet. A little worried, I pulled off my shirt and jeans quickly and crawled into bed behind him, propping myself up on my elbow and wrapping my arm around his waist. After a moment, he put his hand over mine, holding it there as I kissed his cheek gently. We were quiet for a long time before I felt him start to tremble.

"Why does it have to be so fucking hard?" he whispered, his voice breaking. My heart hurt as I pulled him back harder against my chest, holding him tightly. He pulled away almost at once, but I didn't have time to be disappointed before he was rolling over and throwing his arms around me, burying his face in my chest. I felt warm tears against my skin, and I stroked his hair. Normally, when we would lie in bed, I would be in his arms with my head on his chest. Tonight, he needed that comfort, and I held him closely, hoping that he could feel my love for him.

"I don't know, Jamie," I whispered back, continuing to run my fingers through his soft blond hair as he clung to me. I didn't know what else to say, what else I could say. He was right; it shouldn't have to be so hard.

"I hate lying to them. Emma told me tonight that she loves me, and I just... I couldn't say it back. That's crossing a line that I can't do. It makes me sick every time I see her, knowing that I'm just using her." His voice was full of pain and regret. I wanted to comfort him, to tell him that it was something we had to do, but then I remembered the look on Brenda's face after I'd kissed her. She looked like she'd won the lottery, and I would have to be the one to take that away from her. It wasn't fair to them, and it definitely wasn't fair to us.

"Maybe we should start dating other girls, so that they don't get so attached," I suggested, and he snorted humorlessly.

"Why, so we can have more collateral damage?" he asked, his arms tightening almost painfully around my waist as he kept his face pressed tight against my chest. "I'm not going to go to hell because I'm gay. I'm going because I'm a bad person." Shocked at his statement, I pulled back quickly and dislodged him from me. Grabbing his chin, I pulled it up so that his red-rimmed eyes met mine.

"You are not a bad person, Jamie, not even close. You're one of the best people I know, and I won't listen to you talk about yourself like that. I love you, more than I thought I could ever love anyone, and it's because you're kind and generous and loving. If it bothers you, break up with her, and we'll work it out another way. But don't ever say that you're a bad person, because I don't think I would have survived this long without you." Leaning down, I kissed him. It wasn't a sexual kiss, just a slow, sweet expression of just how much I truly loved him.

"I am," he whispered. "When I saw you kissing her, it hurt so fucking bad. I just wanted to pull you away and call her a... well, a bitch. Even though I know she didn't deserve it. She doesn't know how I feel about you."

"I know, Jamie. Believe me, I know."

We lay there in the darkness, clinging to each other until we both fell into fitful sleep.

CHAPTER NINE

"It's just a retreat with a bunch of kids from church. We're going down to the river to camp, swim, and fish. I thought it would be nice to go together. Well, not together-together, but... you know what I mean," Jamie said, throwing his hands up in the air. "Look, it's not uncommon for people to bring friends. To be honest, our youth group pastor has been wondering when I'm going to bring you on an outing. I thought this would be a good time."

"You really want me to go with you?" After the date that I'd made him go on, how could I refuse him this?

"Yes, I really want you to go with me."

"Then I will." I kissed him lightly on the nose, and he grinned.

Later, his words rang in my head as the bus headed out of town on the highway that led to the campgrounds near the Anizati River where we would be spending Friday and Saturday night. According to the youth pastor, Ben, we would be returning home early enough for church on Sunday. God forbid we miss church on Sunday, even for a church activity. The weekend seemed important to Jamie, and after he had agreed to our date despite his legitimate fears, I could certainly hang out with him and the church crowd for a weekend of camping.

Sitting side by side on a bus full of mostly teenage boys, I felt more comfortable with Jamie in public than I had in a long time. We laughed and joked with the guys sitting in front of us. Bobby was going to be a junior at Madison High in the town next to Crayford, and Karl was an incoming junior at Crayford. They had become friends in the youth program and sounded almost as close as Jamie and I. I'm sure they'd been hanging out at church for years, and it was nice that they weren't exclusionary about it, not like the social groups at school. They wanted to laugh and crack jokes with us just like we were a part of their group.

It was nice.

The drive to the campground took just over half an hour, and I started to get excited as we pulled into the lot where they would park the bus. I had never been camping before, and the prospect of doing so, especially with Jamie in the tent beside me, was exhilarating. Even though it was one of the weekends we would have spent Saturday night in the tree house, I didn't feel like I was missing out on anything. We'd talked about it ahead of time and had decided that trying to fool around in the tent would be too risky, but it wasn't always about sex with us; just being with Jamie was enough for me.

We filed out of the bus and lined up single file so they could account for all of us. I wasn't sure if they thought one of us had jumped off the bus while it was in motion, but I guess if you were responsible for twenty or so teenagers, it was better to be safe than sorry. The few girls who had braved the trip, thankfully Emma not among them, stood huddled off to the side. The guys were spread into small groups and anxious to get the show on the road, Jamie and I included. He looked cute in his cutoff jeans and that blue T-shirt that was my favorite on him, his hair wild from the wind blowing through the open bus window. The heat in the bus had been stifling, so his face was a little red, but he still looked perfect to me.

We looked excitedly around the wide expanse of the campsite. The bright blue sky spattered with clouds set off the greenery completely—the shrubs, the trees. It was the picture of beauty, and with the sound of the river flowing in the background, the soundtrack was just right too. They unpacked the minivan where all of our gear was stored, setting the tents, sleeping bags, and backpacks on the ground. We swarmed the stuff, pulling our own gear onto our backs and waiting for further instructions.

"Okay, guys, I need for you to gather around while I give you your lot assignments. I want you to head straight there once you know where you should put up your tent. Build your campsites over the next hour, and then we'll start getting things together to go swimming. After that is lunch, and then we'll go over the evening Bible study itinerary," Pastor Ben said, trying to compete with the excited babble from the rest of the campers.

"Two-twelve... Two-thirteen... Here, Brian, this is us, two-fourteen," Jamie said as we walked along the man-made trail carved through the dense undergrowth. Except for the twenty or so high school kids laughing and fooling around, the campsite had a quiet majesty. It wasn't a commercialized park like some others; there were no advertisements blocking the view of the trees. The only building to be seen was the ranger station, and I'm pretty sure there were no souvenirs to be found there. The founders of the place had taken great pains to keep it natural.

It was beautiful.

The flat, grassy, numbered lots that we were camping in were spread out on either side of the trail with a sort of cul-de-sac at the end, which was surrounded by huge leafy oaks. In the center of the semicircle of lots was a large campfire pit. A few of the chaperones had already begun to gather wood to build a fire before nightfall.

"Howdy, neighbors!" someone called from the next campsite, where Bobby and Karl were setting up their tent. It seemed that they had a little more experience than the rest of us, because in the short time since we'd left Pastor Ben, their tent was almost completely set up.

"Hi, Bobby, Karl," Jamie greeted with a smile. I was happy that we were in such friendly company; since we had started our relationship, we had cut ourselves off from everyone, and I was looking forward to socializing with other people for a while. Briefly, I wondered if that was what Jamie had had in mind when he had invited me on the trip or if it was because he would have missed me as much as I would have missed him.

Pulling out the old tent that Jamie's parents had given us, we organized the pieces on the ground and began to put them together. Jamie's dad had gone through setting it up the night before, making us set it up and take it down three times before he deemed us ready to do it on our own. After all of the practice last night, Bobby and Karl only finished a few minutes before we did. Next, we crawled inside and set up the rest of our equipment, the sleeping bags and snacks.

"You know what this reminds me of?" Jamie asked with a smirk. Looking around at the canvas walls and floor, I shrugged, having no idea what he was talking about.

"Our tree house," he whispered and then leaned forward. The kiss was brief but soft and sweet as he stroked my cheek lightly with his fingertips. "I'm glad that you're here, Brian. I didn't want to come without you and miss you all damned weekend."

"Thank you for inviting me," I told him, realizing for the first time since he'd asked me to go with him that my apprehension was gone. The tension in my stomach had eased, and I was truly happy to be there with him, even though we were with the people who hated gays and told us we were going to burn in hell. I guess there was really no way to avoid interactions with those kinds of people; they made up the majority of our world.

Our lips met in one last tender kiss, and then he sighed and crawled out of the tent. I allowed myself one huge smile, a feeling of triumph in my heart, before I followed him. The rest of the kids were gathering in a clearing near where we had received our lot assignments, laughing and talking. A couple of them were smacking a volleyball around while others were tossing a football. It was a laidback kind of atmosphere that felt very welcoming. We waited for our new neighbors and then headed over.

Pastor Ben went over the rules and precautions of swimming in the river. He made sure to stress that it wasn't like swimming in a pool, that we needed to be aware of the current and be sure we could always see the red flag of the campsite. After about ten minutes of lecturing, he let us go back to our tents to change. It was everything I could do not to watch Jamie, naked next to me in our little tent.

God, I wanted to touch him.

Fortunately, we were both more frightened of what would happen if we were caught than we were aroused. So as much as I wanted to touch or kiss him, or even just hold his naked body against me, I kept my distance. We changed quickly, tossing our discarded clothes into the corner of the tent before heading out to join the others. It was a clear, hot day, perfect for swimming. Pastor Ben said that we would have a couple of hours to swim and relax before dinner.

When we got down there, a couple of guys I hadn't met had started a game of touch football near the bank of the river. They asked Jamie and me to join, but we wanted to get in the water.

"Maybe later," Jamie told them with a grin as we waded out into the river. He was in higher spirits than I had seen him in a while. I wasn't sure if it was due to being with his friends from church or because he was with me, but it didn't matter as long as he was happy.

"Let's go farther downstream away from this mob scene," he said in a low voice, grabbing a discarded Frisbee from the bank. We both reclined back to lie on top of the water, letting the current take us downstream. We stood up several hundred yards away from the group but could still see them. No one seemed to notice or care that we had drifted off.

One of us stood on either bank of the small, fairly shallow river, and we began to toss the disc back and forth. Jamie had made some truly spectacular catches, diving into the water on either side of him in order to grab it. After a while, we were laughing and grateful for the time we got to spend together outside of the sanctuary of our tree house. Nearly an hour later, we were both exhausted from playing in the water against the current. Hiking up the bank, we found an open patch of grass and lay down.

The beads of water glistening on his sun-kissed skin drew every bit of my focus. I watched as the water trailed a gentle, winding path down over his smooth chest. It took every measure of control I possessed not to lick it. Jamie turned onto his stomach, letting the sun warm his back, and I let my eyes wander over his damp skin, soft and supple in the fading sunlight. I followed the lines down his back, his side, until the curve of his hip disappeared into his low-riding swim trunks.

My God, he was beautiful.

I took several deep breaths in an attempt to get my growing erection to calm. It wouldn't be good for someone to stumble upon us, lying less than a foot from each other while I was hard as granite. Desperate, I looked away from Jamie, burying my face in my arms. Lying on my stomach started to get uncomfortable, but I didn't dare turn over.

"I... I think we need to get back in the water," Jamie said in a strained voice. "The water is cold and I... I'm...."

"Me too," I said with a slight chuckle. At least I wasn't alone in my arousal. I was thrilled that I seemed to have the same effect on him, that he was as strongly attracted to me. I loved that I turned him on just by lying next to him in the grass. There was so much I wanted to do to him right now, but there was no way we could take the chance.

"Come on, then." Jamie took my hand for just a minute to pull me up. He held it longer than necessary as we made our way over to the water. I was about to say something, worried that someone would see us, when he finally let go. Once again, we waded in up to our chests, the cool water soothing my hot skin, and I began to calm down. Jamie looked more relaxed as well and started a lazy forward crawl against the gentle current. I waited a moment so that we would not be too close and then followed, Frisbee in hand.

"Okay, guys, dry off and head back to the tents; you have about thirty minutes before dinner," Pastor Ben called to the kids in the water as we rejoined the group.

Dinner consisted of chips, soda, and hot dogs cooked over the open flame of the campfire while Pastor Ben regaled us with tales of his youth trips with a church that he'd attended growing up in Wyoming. I didn't pay strict attention to what he was saying but instead watched the spectacular sunset behind him as he spoke. Sitting on a collapsible camp chair, he was like the elder of the tribe while we sat on the ground looking up at him. Our paper plates sat precariously on our laps as we ate and paid tribute to his storytelling. The day was still warm, so the campfire was largely unneeded except to roast the hot dogs. The purpose it served was one of atmosphere, allowing us to come together as a group, as friends, and bond.

For one night, because of our lies of omission, we were accepted.

After a long, slow, tender kiss goodnight hidden in the confines of Jamie's sleeping bag, I retreated to the opposite side of the tent. For an instant, it felt like banishment, and the sadness flooded through me. When we were lucky enough to be alone together, I was used to sleeping in Jamie's arms. I had to be content to watch his moonlit profile from a distance. Sighing quietly to myself, I lay down in my sleeping bag and watched Jamie as he gazed at me. Lost in each other's eyes, we finally fell asleep.

The next day was full of all kinds of activities that we participated in with the group. We seemed to be accepted by default. Even the social hierarchy that was prevalent at school didn't exist here. The playing field was level. It must have been the "love thy fellow man, if he looks like you" church attitude radiating down from on high. By on high, I meant Pastor Ben, not God.

For once, we weren't even picked last.

"Hey guys, let's get washed up for dinner," Pastor Ben said as our volleyball game came to a quick and decisive end with the spike from our six-foot-three center. We all headed up to the ranger station to wash up. The sense of camaraderie, of a brotherly friendship, a brotherly love, lasted for most of the night.

But as we know, all good things must come to an end.

While we were sitting around the campfire, Bobby told a ghost story, intending to frighten us, but that wasn't the scariest part of the night. One of the other boys, Dale Parks, tripped on a branch in the dark on his way back from the bathroom and landed on Karl, knocking him flat with Dale sprawled precariously on top of him.

"Hey!" Karl shouted at the bewildered Dale while Bobby pulled the boy off of him. "What are you, some kind of fag?"

Of course, I doubted that Karl thought the boy was gay, but he was embarrassed and humiliated by having this guy on top of him. I suspected maybe he was a little aroused by the way Dale had moved against him in an attempt to extricate himself.

"Shut up, of course I'm not a fag. I tripped, you asshole," Dale retorted, his flushed face perfectly illuminated by the firelight. He started toward Karl, and it looked like even though he was smaller, he intended to punch him. Bobby got up and pulled Karl behind him.

"Hey, it was an accident, right? Let's just calm down," Bobby said, putting a hand up to caution Dale from taking things any further. Another boy stood up. I didn't know his name, but his face was alight with mischief and excitement.

"Speaking of fags, did you guys hear about Ray Andrews over in Dalton? Jimmy goes there, and he was just telling us." He spoke quickly, indicating a grinning, mousy, sandy-haired boy at his feet. The rest of the boys stopped what they were doing to listen. Even Karl and Dale backed off and gave the story their attention. "He got caught jacking off in the locker room after gym. Apparently, he liked the sight of all the naked guys." A collective sound of shock arose from the enraptured group. "Yeah, Jimmy said the kid's parents were so ashamed that they pulled him out of school. They're gonna send him to a special school for queers, try to cure him."

"Goddamn fags," Bobby said, sitting back down. "They should all just get AIDS and die, burn in hell like they deserve." The matter-of-fact way in which he said it, the automated, programmed response coming from someone who, until minutes before, I might have considered a friend, made me sick. The worst part was when I looked over and saw Jamie nodding right along with them. As I caught his eye, he gave me a meaningful look, and I started to nod too. Of course we had to nod, of course we had to agree, to belong. Just as soon as I could safely do so, I excused myself from the group and went back to our tent. Jamie and I didn't so much as kiss before going to bed; we just couldn't take the risk.

The next morning, Jamie and I packed in silence. I had never been so relieved to be going home. Richard and Carolyn may have been foster parents, but I always felt safe with them. One wrong step with the brainwashed zealots, and we could have found ourselves drowning in that river. After that boy was tied to a fence in Wyoming, anything could happen to us.

Anything.

"Brian, I'm going to the grocery store tomorrow; have you decided what you want for your birthday dinner?" I was startled out of my musings and looked up as Carolyn continued frying the chicken for supper on the stove.

"I hadn't really thought about it. Whatever you want is fine with me," I told her, somewhat distracted. Earlier in the week, Jamie had also asked about my birthday, only he had asked about a gift. *What more could I want for my birthday than him?* And then it came to me. I knew exactly what I wanted from Jamie for my birthday.

"Carolyn, can we have tacos?" I asked her, knowing that tacos were something very fast and easy to make and eat. I'd be able to get out of the house and over to Jamie's for the night. Neither Jamie's parents nor the Schreibers would take issue with me wanting to spend my birthday with my best friend. Only, they could not know what I was going to ask him to give me for a present.

"Sure, Brian, thanks for making it easy for me," she said with a smile. "Want something quick because you have a hot date?" I almost choked on the soda I was drinking. With effort, I managed not to spew it all over the table.

"No, actually, I was planning to hang out with Jamie," I told her in the most casual tone that I could conjure.

"You spend a lot of time with Jamie, I notice, to the exclusion of anyone else."

Well, if that wasn't a perfect opening. *Why was I so terrified of taking it?*

Carolyn put a large silver cover over the frying pan she was using for the chicken, set the tongs down on the plastic spoon holder next to the stove, and came over to sit down at the table across from me. Her expression was kind as she watched me fidget in my seat. It was almost like she knew that I had something to tell her, but she didn't prod or pressure me, she just waited. I stared at the table, the shiny polished surface reflecting the light from the setting sun shining in through the back door.

"There's something I need to tell you," I said with a sigh, not looking up.

"I might get upset, I might get angry, but you know that I'll still care about you, right?" she asked, dipping her head down to catch my eye. I nodded. Intellectually, I knew that was true, but it didn't make me any less afraid to tell her. I was definitely not ready to be "outed" yet, to be forcibly removed from the safety of my closet where it was nice and dark and comfortable. Everything that I needed was there: my dignity, the respect of my foster parents and friends, and Jamie's love. *What would happen when the door of that closet was opened, with or without my permission, and a bright light was shined on my life, on my relationship with Jamie?* Even though I was only telling her, it felt like I was exposing everything in that closet to the world. Richard had already suspected before he'd brought me into his office to talk. Carolyn would be the first person that I had consciously chosen to tell. It was a huge distinction in my mind, and a deep line in the sand that felt like a chasm.

I took a deep breath.

"I think... No, it's more than that...," I started, fumbling over my words much like I'd fumbled over my words to Richard. Taking another breath, I ripped off the proverbial Band-Aid.

"I'm gay."

I hung my head, unable to look at her. I kept my eyes on the table, preparing myself for the hurtful words that were sure to come. However, to my surprise, the tears didn't fall from my eyes. The secret was out, and there was no taking it back.

"I'm very disappointed in you, Brian," Carolyn said, and not only did her words convey that message, but I could hear it in her voice as well.

"Do you think I wanted this?" I asked incredulously. "Do you think I'm happy being some kind of freak? You can't be any more disappointed in me for being gay than I already am in myself." I started to get up from the table; her disapproval and disappointment were exactly the reason I hadn't wanted to tell her and hurt more than I wanted to admit to myself. I had always considered Carolyn my ally.

"I'm not disappointed in you because you're gay, Brian," she said, and her voice was sharp, angry. "I'm disappointed because you're ashamed of it." I looked at her in surprise. "Since we brought you home, I have tried to teach you that you are someone to be proud of. Being gay, no matter what any of the small-minded people around here have to say, is nothing to be ashamed of. That's the way that God made you, and I doubt that He's ashamed of you." Her voice softened again as I sat back down at the table.

"It's Jamie, isn't it?" she asked with a small smile, and I nodded. "I always wondered... I'm glad that you've found someone that you care about. It's something that I always wanted for you because you've been so alone. I knew the first day you brought him home from school with you that you would be very close. He's a good boy." She patted my hand as she stood up to go back to the stove. All of the fear and the procrastination in telling her were for nothing.

"He is that," I said, a grin on my face since she'd first said his name.

"Are you staying over there on your birthday?" she asked, trying for casual but only achieving mildly curious. I nodded, explaining that the Mayfields had already cleared it if it was okay with her. "It's fine with me. I'm glad that it will be something special for you."

I certainly hoped that it would be special. There was only one thing that I had asked of Jamie for my birthday. He was hesitant, but he hadn't said no. I think he understood that it was the next logical step in our relationship.

More than anything else on earth, what I wanted was for us to make love.

CHAPTER TEN

I stood in the center of the small space alone with Jamie. The shutters that kept out the rain pounding on the roof also kept out prying eyes from our most intimate evening. After setting up two small battery-operated lanterns that cast a warm glow throughout the room, Jamie crawled off of the mattress and stood in front of me.

"Are you sure, Brian?" he asked for what seemed like the twelfth time. My eyes never left his as I nodded. Reaching down, I grabbed the hem of my worn T-shirt and pulled it up over my head. I let it drop to the floor silently.

"I want you to make love to me, Jamie," I told him with no ambiguity in either my voice or the words. He reached down, tentatively grasping the bottom of his tank top. When it was on the floor next to my shirt, he was finally in my arms. As our deep, tender kisses became more impassioned, more heated, I unbuttoned my jeans with trembling fingers. I wanted this. I wanted for us to have that one thing, that one connection that no one could take from us. No one would have as deep a connection with Jamie as I would—not Emma, not anyone.

I needed it.

I needed him.

Hooking my thumbs into the waistband of both my jeans and my briefs, I pulled them down. As I stepped out and straightened up, I felt every bit as naked as I appeared. He knew I was scared, but determined. Looking at me, indecision and fear on his face, he finally undressed, his eyes never leaving mine. Being naked in front of Jamie had aroused me, but the sight of him nude excited me even more. My swollen cock bobbed lightly as he wrapped his thin arms around my waist.

157

Then his lips were on mine, and I forgot to be scared.

"I just don't want to hurt you," he whispered, his forehead pressing against mine as he held me. I could hear the fear in his voice.

"I want to do this," I said, gently taking his face into my hands. "I want to be yours, Jamie, in every way. We are going to go back to school soon, back to pretending, and I need to hold on to this. When I see you walking down the hall holding her hand, I need to know that I have something of you that she doesn't."

Pulling back sharply, he looked at me, but my eyes were on the floor. It was ridiculous to feel that way, after all that we had been through, all that we had done together. While I couldn't explain why it was so important to me, I just knew it was. Perhaps I just wanted to quiet some of the fear, the fear that he would one day leave me.

"You have everything," he said quietly, his voice breaking. The emotions, plainly visible on his face and in his eyes, were staggering. Love, respect, and even a bit of fear were all evident as he kissed me again. I felt his love in every short, heated meeting of our lips, in each tightening of his arms around my waist, and I knew that what he was saying was true. No matter what kinds of odds were stacked against us being together, there was no doubt that he wanted me every bit as much as I wanted him.

"If you don't want to...," I whispered, unable to finish as my disappointment and fear of rejection washed through me. I had been prepared to have sex with Jamie that night, ready emotionally and physically, but I felt the sting of his hedging deep in my chest. With strong fingers, he forced my chin up so that my eyes met his.

"Of course I do," he said, his eyes blazing. "I just don't want us to have sex just to prove something. I want it to happen because of the way we feel about each other."

He wanted me, as much as I wanted him. I crushed myself to him, pressing my face into his neck.

"I love you, Jamie. Please, I want to show you."

Slowly, he nodded, and I turned in his arms and led him over to the mattress. We didn't need roses or candles or anything else to commemorate this moment. There in our sanctuary, by the light of battery-operated lanterns, on an old inflatable mattress, we would become one. We would consummate that promise of forever that I would hold foremost in my heart. No matter what else happened, whether we were discovered or not, we would forever have this moment.

Reaching down into my backpack, I picked up the things that Richard had given me. Jamie's eyes got wide as I set the condoms and lubricant on the floor by the mattress. When he saw them, I think he understood that I was serious about following through. Deep down, I felt guilty and, though I refused to admit it, a little scared about what we were going to do. Only seventeen years old, we were about to have sex outside of marriage; I knew that was a sin. Not only that, we were going to have homosexual sex, which apparently was an even bigger sin. The line we were about to cross was deeply marked in the sand, and we could never, ever go back.

We went to either side of the mattress and crawled naked to meet in the center. Our mouths and our bodies met as we knelt in the middle of the bed, kissing, groping. Falling sideways onto the bed, we lay side by side, and I traced the contours of his perfect face with my fingers. He leaned forward, our lips met, and I wrapped one of my legs around his waist in my desperate need to be closer to him. I stroked his face, his hair, his shoulders, anything that I could reach. We were desperate to be closer. Our perfectly synchronized kisses were punctuated with unrestrained sounds barely discernable above the pounding rain on the tree house roof.

Surprising Jamie by taking the initiative, I pushed him onto his back and straddled his slender hips. I loved the way he looked up at me with a mixture of wonder and lust smoldering in his sapphire eyes. Grasping my hips with his hands as I leaned forward to kiss him again,his hands slid languidly up my sides and into my hair. Whimpering quietly into my mouth, he lifted his hips, rubbing his long, hard cock against mine. His whimpers quickly turned to breathless pants, and slowly I rocked my hips, rubbing against him. My breathing accelerated as well, and I could feel my heart thudding against my ribs.

Moving from his perfect lips, the scent of his body wash mingled with the hot, musky smell of his body as I kissed his neck. My hands shook slightly as I held myself above him, my kisses making a searing, wet trail across his shoulder. His hands moved down, rubbing my back gently as, finally, I kissed my way down his chest. I reveled in the way his nipples responded to my touch, hardening under the careful teasing of my tongue and my teeth. His cock was hard against my stomach.

Reaching down with one hand, he wrapped it around both of our erections and began to stroke them together. The feeling was erotic, decadent, and I shamelessly rocked my hips against his hand. Leaning back, I rested my palms behind me on his thighs, and my head fell back.

"Jamie," I intoned softly as his other hand slid over my stomach and then as high as he could reach on my chest, splayed over my heated skin. Taking one of my hands off of his thigh, I laid it over his hand on my chest, holding it there, and I was sure he could feel my heart pounding under his palm. He sat up, kissing my chest as I continued to roll my hips, thrusting my cock into his hand. Wrapping his other arm around me, his breathing became increasingly labored, and he squeezed my ass, cupping the flesh in his strong hand. I don't think he'd ever been quite so aggressive, but it excited me that I made him lose control.

"Oh God, Brian...," he moaned as I rocked my hips faster, rubbing his cock hard with my own. Pulling back slightly, he put his hand on my hip, stopping my motion. "Lie down on your side."

I looked down at him for just a moment, kissing him deeply before I climbed off his lap. As he had asked, I lay on my side facing him, and he swung his legs around so that they were near the top of the mattress before he scooted forward toward me. I felt him lift my leg, bending it at the knee, before his warm mouth was on the head of my cock. My head rolled back, and my long, strangled moan was loud in the small space. His answering moan made his lips vibrate on my sensitive skin; as I moved myself gently in and out of his mouth, I wrapped my fingers around his shaft and started to stroke him, loving the hardness under his silky skin. Every bit of my shyness, my modesty, was forgotten as I pushed his legs apart.

Taking his sac into my mouth, I sucked lightly as I massaged his inner thighs. It didn't take long before he was squirming, desperately trying not to grind his hips into my face. Several long, tender licks from his balls up to the tip of his cock made his grinding more insistent. The vibrations were getting more intense as he sucked me deeper into his mouth. His mouth was soft and hot, and it felt so fucking good. Grunting around him, I rubbed his ass, squeezing, pulling his cheeks apart and opening him up to me. My body started to tighten, but I didn't want to come; I wanted to wait until Jamie was deep inside me before I let myself go. As I started to pull back, Jamie pulled back hard, jerking his cock out of my mouth.

"Stop... stop," he panted. "I'm going to come if you don't stop."

I felt his hot breath against my leg as he pressed his forehead against my hip, fiercely trying to calm himself down. As his breathing slowed, I felt his loving kisses on my stomach, and he turned his body, pulling me up with him onto the pillows before laying me down tenderly, making me feel like the most important thing in the world to him. Caressing my cheek, he gazed into my eyes, looking for any hint of doubt or hesitation.

He found none.

After one last kiss, he rolled away from me, toward the crate next to the bed. Opening the box, he removed one of the packaged condoms. He rolled on the first one inside-out and then swore. I laughed nervously while he rolled the second one on correctly. The reality of what we were about to do was pounding in my head. The tension in my body was near the breaking point, and sweat beaded on my forehead as I waited for him to be ready.

"How should we...," Jamie began but then trailed off, a little self-conscious. His face and chest were flushed, most likely from a combination of the heat, his excitement, and his embarrassment. I had to remind myself that even though he was older, he had no more experience than I did. Considering the different possibilities that I had seen in the pictures on the Internet, I began to describe what I had seen. I wanted to make things as easy as I could; we were both so nervous.

"You could be behind me? But I...," I started, but then it was me who was embarrassed. It was starting to become a bit awkward, and I didn't want that. I wanted it to be beautiful, special. I wanted it to be perfect.

"But what?" he asked affectionately, pushing my damp curls back and kissing my forehead.

"I want to see your face." He moaned softly, and his mouth moved from my forehead to kiss me, a deep, penetrating kiss. Then he pushed me back against the pillows again and took the lubricant from the crate. Popping the lid, he poured a liberal amount into his cupped palm, spilling a bit on the sheets. First, he generously smeared it over his condom-sheathed cock, and then he nudged my legs apart with his elbows. As he used his long fingers to open me to him, I looked at the rough ceiling of the tree house.

At first it felt strange, even a bit wrong, to have someone, even Jamie, touch me like that. I tensed, and for a few minutes it felt more like an examination than lovemaking. My cock began to soften a little, and when I felt him add a second finger to the first, it started to burn. I felt stretched, invaded. I reached down and grasped myself. While he slid his fingers in and out of my body, I stroked my cock. After a while, it started to feel good. So I tried to stop thinking about the guilt and the fear, focusing only on the pleasure he was giving me.

Planting my feet on the mattress, I pushed up into his hand, my head driving back against the pillows.

"Oh... that feels good," I told him as I spread my legs further.

"Are you ready?" he asked breathlessly, and biting my lip, I nodded. I wanted to tell him so much more in that moment, that I wasn't afraid, that I loved him, but the fear had crept back into my chest, and I felt strangled around my own words.

Getting to his knees, he pushed my legs up, and I held them there as he took his own cock in his hand. Panic threatened to choke me as he guided himself to my opening. I took a deep breath, and my whole body tensed as I felt the head pressing against my anus. As he pushed forward, I closed my eyes, unable to stop the cry that was forced from me by his penetration. Tears formed in the corners of my eyes, and my hands balled into fists behind my knees as I held my legs.

"Are you okay?" he asked worriedly and started to pull out, remorse evident in his tone, but I released one of my legs and grabbed his hip. We'd already crossed that barrier; there was no reason for us to stop now. The pain, which was now shooting up my back, would subside in a few minutes. At least... I hoped it would.

"Just... just give me a minute," I gasped, feeling my anus spasm around his cock. The pain, the burning, was intense, and I tried to stop the tears that were welling in my eyes from falling. Jamie leaned forward, kissing me gently on the forehead. As he remained perfectly still, his muscles straining with the desire to continue, I felt my body start to gradually relax around his invading penetration. Finally, the pain subsided from a sharp burn to a dull ache.

"Please... just go slow," I requested, trying to force my body to relax. When he slowly pushed forward, it felt like I was being split in two. Gritting my teeth, I grunted and clenched my eyes against the pain. As tenderly as he could, he began a very slow pace, his hips moving against mine as he made love to me for the first time. Again and again he pushed carefully, painfully into me. A few of the tears that had been threatening to fall rolled down my cheeks as I continued to stare at the ceiling, trying not to think about the pain and the way this beautiful moment had become so uncomfortable between us.

"Brian," he murmured as he leaned forward, wiping my tears away with his trembling fingers and kissing me. As he did, my legs were pulled higher up on his forearms, and the feeling of him inside me started to change. The burning pain was replaced by a different kind of heat, a heat that started to spread through my entire body. It started to feel good, really good. I wrapped my arms around his shoulders and held him in that position. His damp forehead pressed against my cheek as he stopped moving.

"Right there, Jamie... Just like that... please... please!" I implored as I started to get hard again. My hand wasn't on my cock; Jamie was just touching a place inside me that made me so hard. The pleasure of it coursed through me, making my balls tighten. I didn't know exactly what had changed or why the way he was thrusting into me made it different, but he started to move in earnest now. I moved right along with him, my hips slamming against his of their own volition. Wrapping my legs around his waist, he slid his arms under my shoulders. We were as close as two people could be, and I suddenly understood why people called it becoming one person.

This was what I'd always thought making love was all about.

Grasping my shoulders for leverage, he started to thrust a little harder. I reached down between us and began to stroke myself in time with his thrusts. The feeling was incredible, and I felt as if my heart would burst with the emotion that was coursing through me as we made love. It was beautiful and sweet, and I knew that as long as I lived, I would always remember that night, those precious moments when we were one. I would remember the cadence of the rain as it pounded on the roof, the smell of Jamie's hair as he pressed his forehead into the pillow next to my head, and of course every moan, every grunt, and every whimper that was forced from him in the heat of his arousal.

"Oh... God... Jamie," I whimpered as I felt my orgasm build. My body was on fire, and the increasingly animalistic sounds coming from Jamie told me that he was also close. His head fell back onto my shoulder as I fisted his damp hair tightly with my free hand, just trying to get him closer. I needed him; I needed his love and his comfort.

"Please," I begged, although I wasn't sure what for, while my other hand continued to rub and stroke my erection with frenzied speed. Panting, I felt that bowstring in the pit of my stomach as he drove relentlessly into me. The muscles in my legs, my shoulders, and even my chest and neck tightened. Fuck, I was right there. Finally it snapped, and even over the sound of the fan and the radio, my cry was loud.

"Oh God... God...." I clung to him as I came, the jets of semen trapped between our writhing bodies. I felt myself tighten around Jamie, squeezing his cock inside me. With the added tightness around him, his hips bucked into me, and then he suddenly stilled, his body riding wave after wave of his climax. Crying out into my neck, he kissed it tenderly and then turned his face, pressing his forehead into my shoulder. His breathing was loud and labored in my ear as I wrapped both arms around him. Pulling back slightly, he sought my lips with his own and kissed me sweetly as he held me.

I pushed the guilt back into a corner of my mind. The line was crossed, and there was no way to go back.

"I don't think I've ever felt so close to you," he revealed, his lips finding mine again and again. "I know that I was a little nervous at first, but I wouldn't trade how I feel right now for anything in the world."

"I love you so much, Jamie," I told him between tender kisses.

"I love you too," he replied breathlessly. "Always." He rolled onto his back, throwing the used condom into the grocery bag we used for garbage, and then he pulled me to him. I wrapped my arm around his chest, and one leg over his. Resting my head on his chest, I listened to his heart, still racing a bit as his breathing began to slow. The breeze from the fan felt good on our overheated skin, damp from our exertion. I fell asleep in his arms, never wanting to be anywhere else.

CHAPTER ELEVEN

The scream woke me up.

At first, I thought it was one of the horrific half-remembered dreams about my parents, but it wasn't.

Jamie and I both bolted upright and looked around wildly. After the disorientation and confusion started to clear, we saw Mrs. Mayfield's horrified face, flushed and sweaty, transfixed as she stood at the top of the ladder. Only the top of her worn purple robe with small tufts of her floral nightgown was visible. Reaching down quickly, I grabbed the sheet from where it had been pushed to the bottom of the mattress during the night and jerked it up to cover us both, but it was too late.

The damage had been done.

Jamie's mother had seen us, naked and entwined, sleeping in each other's arms. The early morning sun filtering through the cracks in the closed shutters had been more than enough light to see us by. The silence, broken only by the repetitive grinding of the fan and the monotone of the voice on the radio, swelled in the confining space. I watched as her disbelieving eyes scanned the small space as if she were trying to find some kind of explanation for what she had seen. My heart jumped into my throat when her eyes landed on the bedside crate and the open condom box that was lying there.

The more Mrs. Mayfield paled, the whiter her knuckles became as she gripped the trapdoor opening. For a moment, I thought she was going to be sick or faint, but instead she began to pray. Her voice was low and rhythmic, almost like she was chanting. I caught a few words as she rocked back and forth, her head bowed and her eyes closed....

"Depraved....

My boy....
Your wrath...."

Jamie refused to look at me, no matter how long I stared at him. His terrified face was bloodless and drawn. I couldn't tell in that moment if he was more frightened of God or his mother.

"*Sinners....*
Mercy....
Repentance...."

I wanted to hold Jamie, to tell him that it would be okay, but I knew any display of affection toward him right now would antagonize his mother even further. As I sat there, frozen, terrified for Jamie, I reminded myself that he would be eighteen in about six months. He would be an adult, and there was nothing they could do to him, or to us. Even if they tried to separate us, we would still be together at school. We could get through this if we just held on to each other. This mental reassurance went on for a few more minutes as I tried to tune out his mother's crazed ranting. I had to be strong now, for Jamie. He would need me while he dealt with his parents.

As Jamie continued to tremble next to me, his breathing coming in sharp gasps, I wondered what he must be thinking. *Was he worried about losing his family? Was he scared that they wouldn't love him anymore? Was he worried that his own mother would hate him?*

Only hours before, we had shared something so momentous, so incredibly special, that I felt like I had been fundamentally altered. I was his, and nothing would change that for me. *Would being discovered ruin everything that we had built?* We sat side by side on the mattress, watching his mother's nearly silent chanting. Jamie looked like he was going to hyperventilate, and I tried to take his hand under the sheet where his mother wouldn't see, but he pulled it away. My chest began to hurt as the fear raced through it.

Then, inexplicably, she just... stopped.

She stopped swaying.

She stopped chanting.

As she stood motionless on the ladder, she may have even stopped breathing. Her eyes flashed as she looked up at us. Then, as her features relaxed into an eerie calm, she said, "Breakfast is ready. You boys need to come in and get ready for church."

Without another word, she climbed down the ladder and was gone. It finally registered that she must have called us to breakfast, and when we didn't hear, she had come up to get us. If we had just turned the radio off or dressed before we'd fallen asleep, none of this would have happened. We had been so careless.

"Jamie," I whispered, terrified at his silence, too afraid to look at his face, sure that all I would find was hatred or indifference. As he sat still as stone next to me, the pain in my heart took my breath away.

Then without warning, he threw himself at me, wrapping his shaking arms around my neck, nearly choking me. "Whatever happens, we will be together, Brian. I am not giving you up, not for them, not for anyone. You are everything to me." Tears burned in my eyes as I nodded fervently.

"Forever," I promised.

We got out of bed quickly and gathered our clothes that we'd strewn across the rough floor in our need last night. In the harsh morning light, we dressed side by side, and unbelievably, I found myself admiring his beauty. No matter what happened when we got into his parents' house, he would always be the most beautiful thing in the world to me. I would be proud to stand beside him and weather the storm.

Grabbing our stuff, we headed for the trapdoor, but neither of us had the strength to open it. Not yet.

Standing directly on the worn wood so that we could not be interrupted, we wound our arms around each other. Silently, we held each other, his head on my shoulder as I fought the impulse to take him and run. *If only we weren't still in high school, that might work.* His breathing was still hoarse and uneven, and I wished that I could take away his fear, his heartache. *What would his parents do now?*

Just then, the fan and the radio both stopped. Someone had pulled the other end of the extension cord, the one plugged in on the wall nearest the door. His mother was getting impatient. I was sure she had figured out that we were being emotional and affectionate.

We had stood in each other's arms as long as we dared.

Placing a small kiss on Jamie's forehead, wishing it were more, I stepped back, waiting for him to move, and then lifted the trapdoor. We climbed down the ladder, each step taking us closer to the hellfire and brimstone that certainly awaited us. I wanted to hold Jamie's hand as we faced our fate, but knew it would only make things worse. The thought of running was ever present, foremost in my mind—but I knew that I wouldn't.

We were in this together, whatever the cost.

Jamie stopped me at the back door and looked at me for a long moment, like he was solidifying a picture of me in his mind before he opened the door. He went over the threshold with a determined air, striding purposefully into the kitchen, where his mother was making pancakes.

"Oh, there you boys are," she said in that eerily cheery voice. "Brian, darlin', why don't you go up and get ready in your church clothes while Jamie eats and then you can switch off." She turned back to the stove and continued to mix up batter. I looked at Jamie, and after a brief glance at his mother, he nodded. I hated leaving Jamie in the kitchen alone to face the wrath of his mother, her fear and anger, but I didn't have any other option. I turned and headed for the stairs. I was starting to get very tired of having no options.

As I pulled my clothes off in the Mayfields' tiny second-floor bathroom, I felt the soreness in my body for the first time. I'd been so preoccupied since Mrs. Mayfield's scream that I hadn't realized just how much my body ached from the previous night. Gingerly, I stepped into the shower, the hot water relaxing my sore muscles. As my body calmed, so did my mind, and I couldn't shut the images off, flashes of our lovemaking repeating: the way he brushed my hair out of my eyes, or the way his body tensed as he came, or the way he held me as we fell asleep. After the initial pain, the lovemaking had been beautiful. I felt closer to him than I had at any point since we had met.

It was infuriating that things had gone so badly that morning. I had wanted to wake up in his arms, kissing and talking. I had wanted to tell him how much the night before meant to me. I had wanted, just maybe, to make love again. The one thing I hadn't wanted was for him to have to choose between his family and me. One more year and we would have been gone; no one would have needed to know. After being caught, we would just have to pretend that much more, pretend we'd broken up, pretend that we'd seen the error of our ways, pretend that we weren't in love. Of course they would try to separate us, but no matter what they tried, it wouldn't work. I would do anything for him, including waiting a year so that we could be together.

It hurt to think about the wedge that would surely be driven between Jamie and his family. I was the catalyst for taking away his family, just as mine had been taken from me. As I washed my hair under the pounding spray, I wondered if I should leave him. *I had been scarred and broken by losing my family; would it do the same to Jamie? Would he resent me? What if we stayed together, but our relationship was irrevocably damaged by the fissure with his family? He said that we would be together forever. Would he still love me for better or worse?*

Even if I left Jamie, it wouldn't change his sexual orientation, and that's what his parents would be upset about. It wasn't that he was with me; I think they had always liked me even if I was just the foster kid from down the street. It was that he was gay, an aberration, and a mark against God. He would be a source of humiliation for them and proof of their failure to produce a normal, healthy Christian boy.

I stepped out of the shower knowing that I could never leave him, not when he needed me. Drying off, I looked at myself in the mirror; I felt different. No longer the boy who had climbed up into the tree house, I was a man, and it was time that I started to act like one. Dressing quickly in the church clothes that I had brought, the only ones I owned, I went back downstairs. Jamie was sitting at the kitchen table, a plate of half-eaten pancakes sat in front of him.

His eyes lit up when he saw me, and it warmed me.

Without a word, he stood and carried his plate to the sink. As he passed me to head upstairs, I felt his hand brush against mine in a gesture of comfort, of promise. Sitting down at the table, I watched Jamie climb the stairs. Once he was out of sight, I waited for his mother to confront me. I expected her to tell me that I was endangering her son's soul, or that I was going to ruin his life, or even that she hated me.

She said nothing. She just set a plate of pancakes in front of me with a soft smile and went back to the stove.

Briefly, I wondered if they had been poisoned.

Her strangely upbeat mood lasted through the ride and all the way into the church. Mrs. Mayfield left us to speak to the preacher while we sat with Mr. Mayfield, who looked tired and upset. That's when I realized why she had put on such a happy face. She had wanted to get me there, so the preacher could talk some sense into us, try to scare us out of being gay.

Nothing, not even God, was going to take Jamie from me.

I didn't listen to the sermon that the man was giving; the most I got was the yelling and gesticulating while I waited for our judgment to be rained down on us once we were forced into the preacher's office. I could feel Jamie next to me, and knowing that he loved me got me through the remainder of the service. We never spoke, and we never looked at each other. It would have been too hard not to comfort him if I'd seen the fear and resignation in his eyes.

It amazed me how much my attitude had changed since that first sermon that had scared me so badly. Over the last few months, Jamie's love had become like a talisman inside my heart, protecting me from the fear and the anxiety. Since the crushing weight of hiding from the Schreibers and from Jamie's parents had been lifted, and they all knew the true nature of our relationship, I felt almost free. I could face anything with him beside me, even the wrath of God.

As I had assumed, Mrs. Mayfield led Mr. Mayfield, Jamie, and me back to the preacher's office after the service was over. I didn't even try to resist. It was something that we were going to have to do at some point; we might as well get it over with. The door closed behind us with the finality of a coffin lid being closed over a corpse, and with just as much optimism.

Without being told, Jamie and I took our places in front of the preacher's large worn desk. We were flanked by Jamie's parents; Mr. Mayfield sat closest to me, though he didn't speak. He just sat stoically, waiting for the preacher to speak, as we were all doing. Mrs. Mayfield sat on the very front of her wooden chair, like a star pupil looking for praise from her favorite teacher. I wondered why that praise would mean so much when it would come at the expense of her son.

"Jamie, your mother tells me that you were caught committing an egregious sin this morning. Is that true?" The preacher sat back in his opulent leather chair, tenting his fingers, waiting for a confirmation. The haughty, self-righteous note in his voice made me angry. He had made it sound like we had killed someone.

"No, Pastor Moore," Jamie said confidently, looking up at the preacher with absolutely no fear. My shock gave in to pride in that moment. Just like Jamie, I held my head high because there was nothing wrong with my love for Jamie, and I wasn't going to let him tell me that there was. Apparently, neither was Jamie. He could have just gone along with what they expected him to say, but he admirably refused.

"You weren't caught laying in sin with another boy? This boy?" he demanded, waving at me, astounded to be contradicted. Sitting forward in his chair, he put both palms down on the desk. His moral superiority was going to be tested, and he knew it.

"Yes, sir, I was," Jamie admitted with no hint of shame. "However, I don't believe that my love for Brian is a sin. I believe that God made me the way that I am."

None of us expected the resounding slap that came next. Jamie's mother had hit him across his face, leaving a red palm print on his cheek. I stood, outraged that she would strike him. Jamie held his hand up, cautioning me to hold my temper. My hands balled into fists at my sides.

"How dare you say such a thing, here in front of Pastor Moore, in God's house? How dare you say that God made something that is clearly unnatural?" Mrs. Mayfield raged at her son. Mr. Mayfield, I noticed, remained strangely quiet. "What you were doing was evil, James. It was against God, and you two will not see each other again."

She turned to me. "Boy, I have tried for years to help you. It was a shame what happened to your parents, but maybe it was God's retribution for your nature. I know that this was your doing. You drew him in to your Godless ways, but I won't let you destroy his soul. He was a good boy before he met you, and he will be one again."

Grabbing Jamie's arm, she pulled him from the room, ignoring the preacher's protests. Mr. Mayfield followed, and I stood there, feeling like she'd taken everything that was good about my life with her as she walked out the door.

CHAPTER TWELVE

"Brian, it will just be a few more days until you're back at school," Carolyn said as we sat at the kitchen table. She was peeling potatoes for dinner while I sat staring at the table, picking apart a paper napkin. As she dumped the peeled and cut potatoes into the pan, I started on another napkin. She got up, carrying the pan to the sink.

It had been nearly three weeks since I'd seen Jamie, and the pain in my chest had grown worse with each passing day. I missed him so much. She was right, though; it would be better when I could at least see him every day, even if I couldn't express my love for him, even if we couldn't be alone. The thought gave me some comfort, but not much.

Just one more year, and we could leave, together.

We just had to survive until the end of the school year.

I recited those two lines over and over in my head, holding on to them in my heart.

Setting the pan on the stove, she turned the burner on and came back to the table. "It won't be too much longer before you boys are eighteen, and then no one will be able to keep you apart. Whether you go off to college or get a job somewhere, you'll be together. It will be all right, Brian, you'll see." I agreed, but when you're seventeen, a year feels like forever. I was impatient, and I wanted Jamie.

Richard came in the back door then, shaking off the rain, but rather than taking off his shoes or setting down his briefcase, he came straight to the table where we were sitting. He was uncharacteristically hesitant when he looked down at me. A strong feeling of unease began to grow in my stomach the longer he didn't speak. Finally, he set his bag down on the table and put his hand on my shoulder.

"Brian, on my way home today, I saw...." He sighed. "I saw a moving truck at the Mayfields'. There was a For Sale sign in their front yard."

No! I screamed the word in my head, trying hard not to let it escape from my lips. *It wasn't possible. There had to be an explanation.*

My hands started to shake, and that uneasy feeling in my stomach turned to nausea. *They couldn't take him away from me, they just couldn't. It wasn't possible. He was the only one on earth who loved me. Without his love, I was nothing. I'd already lost my parents, the ones who were supposed to always be there.* My chest ached, and I found it hard to breathe.

How could God take him too?

Didn't fucking karma owe me one?

I tore out of the kitchen through the back door, barely leaving it on its hinges, and I ran faster than I had ever thought possible. I vaulted over low hedges and scaled fences rather than detouring down alleys. My only thought was getting to Jamie. I didn't know what I thought I could do to stop them, but I had to see him. The shocked looks of people who I nearly knocked to the ground as I ran right past held no interest for me.

As I rounded the corner onto Jamie's street, I saw the moving truck pull away from the curb. It was a huge blue semi truck, big enough to hold the contents of their entire house. *Oh God, it was true.* I screamed, unable to stop the wounded sound from being torn from me. I didn't care who could hear me; I didn't care who else was on the street watching them leave with sick fascination.

It wasn't possible. He couldn't be gone.

The front door of the Mayfield house banged open, and Jamie came running out, no doubt having heard my scream. He threw his arms around me and just kept saying over and over, "I'm so sorry, I'm so sorry." Both of his hands were fisted in the back of my hair, holding my face against his shoulder. I couldn't bring myself to pull back to look at his face; the heartbreak in his voice was staggering. He was shaking with the sobs he was trying hard to contain. I closed my eyes and just held him, trying to memorize his scent, the feeling of him in my arms, the sound of his low breathing. Soon, too soon, I would have nothing.

His father came down the steps, and I watched him walk toward us with a slow and heavy gait. It was evident that he didn't want to leave, but as he passed us on the walk, he said, "You have five minutes, son, and then we need to be on our way. We have a very long drive ahead of us." The fear and pain ripped through me, and I gripped him tighter.

"Where?" I asked, nearly choking on the word.

"San Diego," he whispered. "My father requested a transfer, and it came through last week. They wouldn't let me see you to tell you. I tried to get out, but I couldn't." The emotion finally broke through, and his voice was soon heavy with sobs. I held him tighter, trying to find some measure of comfort for us, but the effort was wasted.

"Jamie, it's time to go," Mrs. Mayfield called from the car, obviously trying to avoid a scene. Two boys holding each other on the front lawn was attracting attention that she apparently didn't want. I didn't know what the fucking difference was if she was moving halfway across the country. She could wait.

"I'll find you," I told him, my breath catching on the last word. He nodded, even though we both knew how difficult it would be to keep my word. My hands clutched at his shirt as my hair became plastered to my forehead. He pushed it away and then, to my surprise, kissed me right there on his front lawn. Desperately our lips met over and over before he pulled away.

I was terrified now. It was all I could do to keep from screaming. Their house was packed, and they were taking him and leaving. They may as well tear open my chest, which may actually have hurt less than them taking my Jamie. I wanted to run, to take him and hide. My panic swelled as he pulled back a little further.

"Never forget that I love you," he said softly, just above the sound of the rain, before he turned and walked to the car. My knees gave out before he had reached the sidewalk, and I landed heavily on the grass. Climbing into the back seat, he turned and watched me as his father pulled away from the curb.

Then a horrible thought came to me, one that burned the hole in my chest caused by his departure. I hadn't told him I loved him. He told me never to forget, and I didn't tell him. I screamed his name into the rain, begging the car to stop, for him to come back. But he was gone.

I sat with my back against the hastily erected For Sale sign, feeling the rain mingle with the tears as he left me, taking every bit of my hope, my joy, and my life with him.

EPILOGUE

Emma Mosely stood rooted to the sidewalk, just two houses away from her boyfriend's house. The note declaring her love for him was clutched tightly in her right hand. When her mother had told her at the beginning of the week that Jamie's family was moving to California, she had been devastated. Running out of her house, she had ended up on Jamie's front porch sobbing to an equally upset Mrs. Mayfield. Jamie's mother told her that she was sorry they had to move, but that his father had been transferred. There was nothing they could do. After several minutes, Emma was able to get a hold of herself, and she asked to see Jamie. Mrs. Mayfield went up to get him, but he refused to come down. *They only had days left to be together, and he refused to see her?*

Then the rumors started to reach her.

She called Jamie every day, but Mrs. Mayfield told her in a polite, embarrassed tone that he was busy or he wasn't home. Emma couldn't understand why Jamie was acting like this. The rumors about him and Brian McAllister couldn't be true; she had kissed Jamie. He certainly wasn't gay. It was ludicrous. The only explanation she could come up with was that he was as devastated as she was about him leaving. So she decided to tell him how she felt. She was in love with him, and she could wait until college for them to be together. It would be hard, but they could apply to the same college, and in just a year, they'd be able to start their life together.

As Emma stood, frozen, watching the exchange between Jamie and Brian, their words were drowned out by the pouring rain. It didn't matter; she had a pretty good idea what they were. Then, just to drive home the point, Jamie grabbed Brian in a way that he had certainly never done with her, and he kissed him. The pain in her chest took her breath away. The rumors were true.

Jamie had used her.

Jamie had lied to her.

Jamie was gay.

The bile rose up in her throat, and she felt like she might be sick. As she watched, Jamie walked to his parents' car and got in the back, never even sparing her a look. He had eyes only for Brian, who sank down next to the For Sale sign in the yard and cried.

No! It should be her crying. It should be her that Jamie kissed before leaving. It should be her that Jamie loved. What they were doing was against God, against nature. God would make them suffer His wrath; He would have His vengeance.

And so would she.

Don't miss out!

Visit the website below and you can sign up to receive emails whenever JP Barnaby publishes a new book. There's no charge and no obligation.

https://books2read.com/r/B-A-EBYTC-IZDIF

BOOKS 2 READ

Connecting independent readers to independent writers.

Did you love *Enlightened*? Then you should read *Aaron*[1] by JP Barnaby!

I can't describe what it's like to want to scream every minute of every day.

Two years after a terrifying night of pain destroyed his normal teenage existence, Aaron Downing still clings to the hope that one day, he will be a fully functional human being. But his life remains a constant string of nightmares, flashbacks, and fear. When, in his very first semester of college, he's assigned Spencer Thomas as a partner for his programming project, Aaron decides that maybe "normal" is overrated. If he could just learn to control his fear, that could be enough for him to find his footing again.

---

1. https://books2read.com/u/meaLgV

2. https://books2read.com/u/meaLgV

With his parents' talk of institutionalizing him - of sacrificing him for the sake of his brothers' stability - Aaron becomes desperate to find a way to cope with his psychological damage or even fake normalcy. Can his new shrink control his own demons long enough to treat Aaron, or will he only deepen the damage?

Desperate to understand his attraction for Spencer, Aaron holds on to his sanity with both hands as it threatens to spin out of control.

Read more at www.jpbarnabyauthor.com.

Also by JP Barnaby

Little Boy Lost Series
Enlightened

The Survivor Series
Aaron
Ben
Spencer
Anthony
Sophie

Watch for more at www.jpbarnabyauthor.com.

About the Author

Let's get real. Yes, JP Barnaby is an award-winning romance author whose Survivor Series was heralded as one of USA Today's favorites. But what you should really know is that JP is a mental health advocate. She writes about all kinds people with mental health issues because the conversation needs to be had—out loud. Depressed people fall in love. Anxious people fall in love. Schizophrenics fall in love.

Everyone deserves to fall in love.

On a side note, JP fell in love with a super chill guy who loves her, not despite all her rips and creases but because of them. So does her 70-lb Staffy, only she does it with more fur.

Read more at www.jpbarnabyauthor.com.

9 798230 700784